"I can't control myself around you."

Philip shrugged, then continued. "You saw what happened on the show this afternoon. I burned a tenderloin, then had to kiss you because it was your fault."

Carrie's eyes widened. "My fault?"

His gaze met hers over the rim of his wineglass. "Yes, of course. I was distracted by your breasts."

Carrie cocked her head and smiled. "Back to those again, are we?" She stood. "Do you mind if I work while we talk?" she asked, thinking that a change of subject was in order. Before she did something stupid like lean forward and kiss him again.

Philip swiftly swallowed the drink in his mouth, set his wineglass aside and hurriedly stood. "Better still, how about I help you?"

Carrie grinned. "Oh, I don't know. I'd hate for you to get *distracted*."

"I should be fine as long as you don't take off your shirt," Philip said casually.

Carrie did ut one second she'ed, and the next, sh and slowly—del her head.

The die was cast.

Blaze™

Dear Reader,

Well, this is it—the last book in my CHICKS IN CHARGE series. I hope that you've enjoyed getting to know these feisty women—and their fantastic heroes—as much as I have. Saying goodbye to them brings a sense of accomplishment tinged with the ultimate regret that I won't be hanging out with them anymore. Like all my characters, they've become friends of sorts, if only in my imagination. If you're just picking up this book, then I hope you'll visit eHarlequin.com and get the others. *Getting It!* was a January release, followed by *Getting It Good!* in February. *Getting It Right!* was on the shelves last month. (Noticing a theme here?)

During the holiday season it's easy to get caught up in shopping, baking and various parties. I don't know how it is at your house, but at mine the bulk—translate *all*—of the work gets firmly placed in my lap. I put up the tree, hang the decorations, do all of the shopping, wrapping and coordinating of schedules. I bake—and typically gain five pounds—and distribute all of our family Christmas cards. But somewhere in the midst of the madness, I always find a few hours to slip away and curl up with a good book. Here's hoping you do, too, and that your season is brimming with lots of girl power and romance.

Happy reading!

Rhonda Nelson

GETTING IT NOW!

Rhonda Nelson

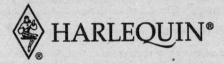

HARLEQUIN®

TORONTO • NEW YORK • LONDON
AMSTERDAM • PARIS • SYDNEY • HAMBURG
STOCKHOLM • ATHENS • TOKYO • MILAN • MADRID
PRAGUE • WARSAW • BUDAPEST • AUCKLAND

This book is dedicated to the *ultimate* Chick in Charge, my phenomenal editor, Brenda Chin. I'm continually amazed and humbled by your infinite wisdom and unending enthusiasm for my work. You are, without question, *the best* editor any author could ever hope to have, and working with you is not only a dream come true, but a blessing that has enriched my life in too many ways to count. My sincerest thanks always.

ISBN 0-373-79227-1

GETTING IT NOW!

Copyright © 2005 by Rhonda Nelson.

This edition published by arrangement with Harlequin Books S.A.

www.eHarlequin.com

Printed in U.S.A.

Prologue

ONLY THE FOUNDING MEMBERS of Chicks in Charge wouldn't think anything about hosting a baby shower at a bar, Carrie Robbins thought with a small smile as she watched her friend open yet another gift. Colored pacifiers floated in margarita glasses—the mom-to-be's a virgin margarita, of course—and baby bottles doubled as candle holders, illuminating New Orleans' Blue Monkey Pub with a properly festive glow.

Though hardly conventional, they'd rented the pub for the night and the small party was an unequivocal success. She popped a petit-four into her mouth and swallowed a sigh of satisfaction as the sugary pastry melted on her tongue.

And the food wasn't half bad either, Carrie thought with a slightly smug grin.

"You've outdone yourself, darling," Frankie said, polishing off another helping of blueberry bread pudding, one of Carrie's signature dishes. "Let me pay you for the food."

"Absolutely not." One of the only perks to parading half-naked around the set of *The Negligee Gourmet* was the paycheck. She'd made a decent living prior to joining the lineup at *Let's Cook, New Orleans!,* but the added cash and security she'd garnered through the slight change in profession had certainly had its advantages. Being able to cater Zora's baby shower without sparing any expense was certainly one of them. Moving out of an apartment and into a house was another.

"Are you sure?" Frankie persisted. "I don't—"

"I'm sure," Carrie told her. She cocked her head, flashed an impish smile. "Cooking in the buff pays well."

Frankie chuckled softly. "Stop belittling. You aren't in the buff." She frowned, evidently searching for a kinder description. "You're merely…scantily clad."

Carrie rolled her eyes. "And painted and teased up like a porn queen," she added dryly. She hadn't counted on that part when she'd signed on with the network, otherwise she might have reconsidered…but she doubted it.

Frankie made a moue of understanding. "I do

wish they'd lay off the makeup and the eighties hair-style. You're gorgeous without all of that."

Her lips curled with droll humor. "I'll be sure and pass your suggestions along."

Not that they'd be heeded. None of hers certainly had. Evidently the male demographic liked sophisticated meals prepared by trashy-looking women. Red lipstick, electric-blue eye-shadow, false eyelashes and big-ass hair seemed to be the perfect combination. Carrie snorted. It invariably took her half an hour to remove the paint and get the various gels, sprays and tangles out of her hair.

Other than the regular trim to remove dead-ends, Carrie didn't have what one could call a hair regimen. She washed, she dried, she brushed. Occasionally she'd braid, but that was the extent of her hair concerns.

As for makeup, she didn't like the feel of it against her skin—too sticky—and other than a sheer gloss on her lips and the rare swipe of a mascara wand upon her lashes, she didn't fool with it. Sitting for a full hour and a half while the hair and makeup people on set painted and poofed her was an excruciating waste of time.

But her friends had been right—it was definitely preferable to working for Martin. Calmly giving that sanctimonious, controlling, petty, ball-less bastard her two-week notice had been, unquestionably, one of the high points in her life.

Had his restaurant not enjoyed world-renowned success, she would have never tolerated his maniacal abuse for as long as she had. But despite his notoriously bad temper, or perhaps as a result of it, Chez Martin's had been the best game in town and she would have been foolish to quit before something better had come along.

Thankfully it had, and she'd happily quit. Martin had gaped like an out-of-water guppy for a full ten seconds before he'd exploded in anger. After everything he'd done for her? How dare she?

Ha.

Other than joyously giving her a hard time for the past several years, she'd like to know just what it was in particular he thought that he'd done for her. Was she supposed to be thankful for the constant criticism? The unpaid overtime? The snide comments about her looks?

Supposedly beautiful people were given preferential treatment in today's society, but all Carrie had ever gotten for her so-called "blessing" was grief, and any time she'd ever shared that—usually in her own defense—she'd been given the whole mockingly snide poor-little-pretty-girl spiel. Not from her real friends, of course. They knew her better.

Still…being attractive wasn't all it was cracked up to be. Men habitually hit on her, underestimated her, and assumed that being pretty somehow made her stupid. Women tended to dislike her on sight, were threatened by her. She had the same insecurities and hang-ups as anyone else. To think that she somehow had it easier simply because of the way she looked was retarded. Hell, everyone had problems.

Furthermore, Carrie had technically been on both sides of the fence. As a child she'd been plagued with a weight problem. Growing up all over the globe with her traveling doctor parents had made it somewhat tolerable—frankly, in her experience people of other cultures were less inclined to make fun of her—but the first time she'd set foot in a U.S. public school, in the latter part of her junior year of high school, had been a different matter altogether.

She'd been taunted, teased and ridiculed until the idea of carrying one extra pound on her frame had been intolerable. She'd gone on a strict diet, had started an exercise regimen, and by the time she'd entered her senior year, she'd shed more than fifty pounds.

Then the "pretty" problems started. She couldn't win for losing.

At any rate, Carrie knew she was healthier and, learning to take control of her food instead of being ruled by it had led to a love of cooking which had steered her into her chosen career path. Who knew who or what she might have been otherwise?

It was ironic really, Carrie thought, idly sipping her drink. Her entire adult life she'd wanted to be taken seriously as a chef. Out of the limelight, in the kitchen—the back of the house, as those in her profession liked to say—letting her food speak for itself, and yet here she was capitalizing on the very thing that she'd always tried to avoid—her looks.

The show had been a huge success, the powers that be were ecstatic. Furthermore, though they'd primarily been targeting the male demographic, recent polls indicated that she was doing well with the female viewers as well. By all accounts, everything about it had been a resounding coup…and if she murmured one word of discontent she'd be that "poor little pretty girl" again, only this time they could add "famous" into the mix. Carrie sighed.

In truth, she didn't give a damn about either—she just wanted to cook.

April Wilson-Hayes slid onto a barstool next to her and gestured to the enormous pile of gifts accumulating on the table beside Zora. "Good thing Frankie made sure the guys were here, otherwise we'd have a hell of time getting all of this stuff loaded into Zora's car."

Another perk to hosting the shower in the bar. Carrie's gaze slid to one of the pool tables on the other side of the room. Ben, Ross and Tate—the proud papa—were currently engrossed in one of many informal tournaments. Though Ben was the newcomer—Ross and Tate had been friends for years—he'd been easily welcomed into the fold. Evidently being married to a CHiC founding member formed an instant commiserating bond of friendship between them.

Carrie could still remember the first time April had brought Ben to one of their weekly get-togethers. Once the pleasantries were over and the first round was finished, Tate and Ross had smoothly summoned Ben aside, presumably to give him a few lessons regarding the care and feeding of a Chick In Charge. Carrie felt a smile tease her lips.

"They're good for lifting heavy objects," Carrie conceded.

And in her opinion, that was about it.

Aside from one serious but soured relationship she'd had in culinary school, she'd yet to find a guy who was genuinely interested in anything beyond her immediate packaging.

Admittedly being the last CHiC without a rooster—Frankie's nickname for the guys—seemed a little odd and she'd be lying if she said she wasn't envious—

hell, who didn't want to be loved?—but until she found the right one—one who would *want* to look beyond the surface, who wouldn't be intimidated by her skill and shared some of the same interests—she wasn't settling. Life was too short and despite wishing she could host her show fully clothed, she was too content to settle for anything less than the best.

Her parents had provided an excellent example—forty years, a few bumps, yet their commitment to each other had never wavered. That's what she wanted, Carrie thought. A love that would endure. They were presently in Africa—along with her younger brother who had also joined the organization—but Carrie couldn't begrudge them their calling. So long as there was a place in the world with little to no medical service, she knew her only sibling and parents would be there.

"Still enjoying the house?" April asked.

"Oh, God yes," Carrie told her. April's husband Ben had been looking for a buyer for his house around the same time she'd inked her *Negligee* contract and she'd wanted out of her claustrophobic apartment and into a home with a roomy kitchen.

The stars had aligned perfectly in her favor and to say that she'd fallen in love with the classic Georgian mansion was a vast understatement. It was a little big for one person, but she'd filled it with a collection of antiques and mementoes which had quickly morphed it into her home.

As with most women who are in the market for a house, the kitchen had been the key selling point. Despite all the fancy crown molding and pocket doors, the kitchen remained her favorite room.

"Great," she said with a happy now. "What about work?" April wanted to know. "Any news on that special yet?"

Carrie tensed and shook her head. The special in question was the network's way of capitalizing on their hottest stars and low summer ratings. They'd decided to pair their *Negligee Gourmet* up with Britain's handsome answer to Emeril Lagasse—Philip Mallory.

A soft sigh stuttered out of her lungs. Unfortunately she couldn't think his name without summoning the image and…mercy. Thick, wavy dark-auburn hair, pale gray eyes—liquid silver, she thought—and a six and half foot athletic frame that put a woman in mind of crisp white sheets, a dark stormy night and warmed truffle oil. Excellent bone structure, a crooked, boyishly sexy smile and that biting British wit made him one of the most compelling men she'd ever shared air with.

Unfortunately, it was quite obvious that he didn't enjoy sharing air with her.

Carrie didn't know if he'd merely taken an instant dislike to her, or if it was her show that he held in such distain. Given the slight sneer his otherwise beautiful lips usually formed when he saw her and the blatant disregard he generally treated her to the very rare occasions their paths crossed, she imagined it was a little bit of both.

Ordinarily she wouldn't have given a damn—she'd developed a pretty thick skin over the years and working with Martin had certainly toughened her hide, but Philip's ready uncharitable opinion of her stung more than she'd care to admit. Probably because she'd always nursed a secret crush and, more important, admired him as a peer. To know that evidently neither sentiment was returned was quite a blow to her ego, not to mention wholly disappointing.

She'd been watching him for years—she'd faithfully followed his British program before he'd made the hop across the pond—and, though at the time she'd formed her opinions she'd never met him, she would never have thought he would have ended up being so…shallow.

Finding herself slightly starstruck and still gallingly attracted to him only added insult to injury.

Between being extremely cautious and adhering to exacting standards, Carrie had always found it relatively easy to master her libido. Quite frankly, it took a special guy—the perfect ratio of confidence, intelligence, humor and sex appeal—to do it for her and very few men made the cut.

Regrettably, aside from being a judgmental ass, Philip Mallory *defined* her perfect guy. Had from the first instant she'd watched him in the kitchen.

Everything about him called to her, evoked her senses. That crisp accent, the self-deprecating humor. He frequently referenced books or opinions that she shared and she'd always foolishly imagined some sort of special link, an "if-only…" fantasy where, were they to ever meet, there'd be this instant recognition. Sort of like Meg Ryan and Tom Hanks in that final scene of *Sleepless in Seattle*. Carrie's lips curled. Clearly she'd been watching too many romantic comedies, but that didn't change the fact that she'd found herself seriously intrigued and attracted to him.

And who wouldn't be? He was positively gorgeous.

Particularly his hands, Carrie thought, easily summoning the shape—the strength—of them to her mind. Watching him work… Ah, she thought as a soft smile shaped her lips, now that was art in motion. Simply beautiful.

But watching him work *with her* would be her worst nightmare—a *waking* one if the execs had their way.

Number one, she knew that he'd been resisting the idea for months, that he was vehemently opposed to working with her. Carrie inwardly cringed. Talk about humiliating. She'd been thrilled at the idea and he'd been appalled, had evidently equated the proposal with begrudgingly walking his annoying little sister to school. At least that was the rumor in the kitchen and he'd definitely not given her any reason to suspect otherwise.

Considering that her entire body went into sensory overload every time she heard that voice or caught a glimpse of him, Carrie had no desire to further her humiliation by allowing him a peek at her pathetic attraction, one she was relatively certain she didn't have a snowball's chance in hell of concealing if she had to work with him on a day-to-day basis.

She'd like to think that her pride would prevent her from making a fool of herself, but she grimly suspected the combination of her acute fascination *with* him and red-hot attraction *to* him would burn up any vestiges of self-respect. Factor in her penchant for casting him as the lead in her perfect-guy fantasy and things became considerably worse.

In short, Philip Mallory was her Achilles heel.

And if that special became a reality she'd undoubtedly be buying a nice pair of combat boots.

1

One month later…

"BLOODY HELL." Philip Mallory bit out the words. "This cannot be happening again."

"I realize that on the surface it might seem like a recurring scenario, but things are different this time."

Philip glared across the table at his agent. "How so?" he asked sarcastically, sprawling against the back of his chair. "Once again after working my ass off on my own show, I'm being paired up with a talentless hack whose only redeeming quality is a pair of perky breasts."

Hardly an accurate assessment of Carrie Robbins's skill or breasts, but at the moment he was more interested in being pissed off and petty than fair. As far as talent went, Philip knew she was a damned fine chef. He'd watched her show and had frequented Chez Martin's enough to know that she didn't abide mediocre work.

Furthermore, Philip thought broodingly, her breasts were more than perky—they were perfect. Plump, pert and lush. God knows he'd seen enough of them to know over recent months. Between his own acute fascination of her, the skimpy little negligees she wore on set and one smitten cameraman whose zoom lens had a tendency to tighten and stick to her delectable cleavage, he'd been left with little choice. Hardly a hardship, he knew, but Philip was of the opinion that cleavage and nighties were more appropriate clothing for a bedroom than a kitchen. His lips quirked.

Unless, of course, a couple was playing the wicked lord and naughty scullery maid, then her limited attire would be completely fitting. If he didn't think that she was making a mockery of the art of cooking, was selling herself short and not The Enemy—thanks to the cork-brained producers who'd come up with the jolly idea of special programming—Philip wouldn't resent fantasizing about bending her beautiful ass over the nearest counter and taking her until his ruddy dick exploded.

As it was, he did resent it.

Factor out his unfortunate over-the-top attraction to her and it was a too-familiar scene which had once before resulted in a miserable outcome.

"They're not suggesting making it permanent,

Philip. They just want a week-long segment to take advantage of sagging summer ratings."

"I don't give a damn. I'm not doing it."

Rupert winced, causing an unpleasant sensation to commence in Philip's belly. He knew that look. It was the *you're-fucked* look. "Well, see, the thing is—"

"I'm not doing it, Rupert," Philip said threateningly.

"Then you'll be in breach of contract and they'll fire you."

And there it was, Philip thought with a bitter laugh. The bend-over order. "If *I'll* be in breach of contract, then *you* didn't do *your* job and *you'll* be the one getting fired, my friend."

Rupert shifted uneasily and a gratifying flicker of fear raced across his face. It was an empty threat, of course. Rupert Newell represented the longest relationship he'd ever had in his life and he wasn't about to sever it over something as trivial as having to do a week-long segment with *The Negligee Gourmet*. Still…

"How could you have let this happen again?" Philip demanded pleadingly. "After the Sophie debacle, Rupert? Come on!" It was ridiculous.

"I was assured that it would be a nonissue, and you were harping at me to 'make something happen.'" He affected a wounded look, one Philip had seen many times over the years. "So I did, and this is the thanks that I get. Just a year ago I was the best agent in the world for negotiating this deal and now I'm on the brink of getting fired all because of a simple one-week special that in no way resembles the hostile takeover of your show that Sophie-the-whore managed to maneuver."

There was nothing hostile about the way she'd maneuvered *him,* Philip thought, cheeks burning with renewed humiliation. She'd shagged him literally and physically right out of a show. Thanks to a back-door clause which enabled the network to suspend his contract unless he agreed to do "special segments" and a morals clause which prohibited any sexual relationships between currently contracted persons, Philip had found himself screwed—rather poorly, he thought with a moody scowl—right out of a job.

Sophie had insidiously worked her magic behind the scenes, discrediting him as a host, then had cried sexual harassment as the final coup. Despite excellent ratings, he'd found himself summarily fired and Sophie—a sous chef from the kitchen who'd been angling to host—had gotten his show.

Hell, the bitch had even been given *his* set.

By the time Rupert had negotiated the *Let's Cook,*

New Orleans! deal he'd been desperate to get back to work and, while he'd entertained several offers from various schools and restaurants both in the States and the U.K., Philip had ultimately decided against them. He truly enjoyed being in front of the camera—the combination of drama and teaching. Had known that he'd found his niche.

Furthermore, he'd decided a change in scenery had been in order and had found America to his liking. He'd visited often enough before—mostly New York and L.A.—but something about the dark, soulful spirit of New Orleans really appealed to him. Far removed from his rolling English hills, that was for sure.

Since moving here a little over a year ago, Philip had still found a couple of weeks here and there to fly home. He had no family left to speak of—both his parents had passed away years ago, and his only sibling had preceded them in death when she'd been five. A drowning accident, one his parents had never recovered from.

Rather than loving the child they had left, both of them had distanced themselves from him, presumably, Philip thought, to lessen the pain should another unexpected death occur. Philip didn't blame them—couldn't because he'd powerlessly witnessed their grief—but it was years into his adulthood before he'd come to terms with their cohabiting abandonment. They might have lived in the same house, but after Penny's death they hadn't been there for him. They'd been emotionally unavailable. Philip grimaced.

Unfortunately, that continued to be a running theme in his life.

Were it not for his little seaside villa on the Isle of Wight—his ultimate refuge—Philip wouldn't have any reason to board another transatlantic flight. As it was, he could only go a few months before the tug of the small island pulled at him and he found himself gasping for a breath of fresh salty air.

Granted he could get that at any seaside location, but something about the little island had always been home to him. His villa sat on a rocky rise and overlooked a gorgeous view of the ocean. Mornings would find him kicked back in a patio chair with a good book—he'd amassed an extensive library there—and a hot cup of coffee. Philip frowned. Given the present mess he found himself in, he wouldn't mind being there now.

"I've got to let them know something this afternoon," Rupert said. "Since you've been the holdout, they're waiting until they attain your cooperation before discussing it any further with Ms. Robbins."

Philip snorted. "Until they force my cooperation, you mean."

"What do you want me to tell them?" Rupert asked. "I can go back to the table and talk some smack—I have for the past six months—but I don't expect it will do any good." He signed for the bill and stood. "Let me know what you want me to do."

"T-talk some smack?" Philip repeated, an unexpected laugh breaking up in his chest.

Rupert fussily straightened his coat. "It's a new slang term I've learned." He sighed and gave a little whirling motion with his hand. "When in Rome, you know."

"We're not in Rome. We're in New Orleans."

"I realize that."

Philip smothered a snort. "And you're British," he pointed out.

"I'm quite aware from which country I hail," Rupert snapped testily. "I just want to have a better grasp of American jargon. Speak to them in terms they'll understand."

Philip chewed the inside of his cheek, debated the merit of pointing out that the official language of the United States was *English*. Ultimately, he decided against it. Listening to Rupert mangle American slang with that British accent would be a fun source of entertainment in the coming weeks.

And he was going to need as much of that as possible.

"Tell them I'll do it." Philip finally relented. "One week. Her set, not mine—I don't want mine tainted with what I'm certain is going to be a bloody disaster—and I want an addendum added to my contract making my cooperation regarding these damned specials null and void."

Rupert smiled. "Now that's more like it. Peace out," he said, then turned neatly on his heel and left.

Ha, Philip thought, quaffing what was left of his drink. For the next week he seriously doubted he'd be having any sort of peace, in, out, or otherwise.

Furthermore, if he was going to be thrust into this unwanted hell, then he was going to be in charge.

And the sooner *The Negligee Gourmet* knew it, the better.

"UNTIL NEXT TIME, best wishes for *your* hot dishes," Carrie said, her sign-off line. The producer called it a wrap, her cue to let her fixed smile fall.

"Dibs!" Jake Templeman, one of the camera guys called before any of the other behind-the-scenes help could lay claim. A bit of good-natured grumbling ensued amid the crew, but ultimately they let it slide.

Jake hustled up with a to-go box and started plating the meal Carrie had just fixed. "I love eggplant parmesan," he said. He shot her a sly look. "There's enough here for two," he said predictably. "Wanna join me?"

He got points for persistence if not originality, Carrie thought, biting the corner of her lip to hide a smile. She'd been hearing the same line for months—and always answered the same way. "Sorry, not tonight."

Jake cocked his head and grinned, released a quiet dramatic sigh. "You wound me."

She doubted it. Though gorgeous and charming, Jake had worked his way through every willing woman at the network. From what she'd heard and observed he had the emotional capacity of an amoeba. She smiled at him. "You'll live."

"So cold," he said, affecting a shiver, but accepted another refusal with cavalier grace.

"Beautiful show, Carrie," Joyce, her producer told her. "Great job."

Carrie smiled her thanks, released a small breath and resisted the urge to use her apron to start wiping the makeup off her face. She'd done that once before and had ruined what was evidently a pretty pricey accessory. She knew she should be a little repentant, but couldn't summon the sentiment. If they were stupid enough to tie a silk apron on to her, then they'd have to live with the consequences. She could have just as easily ruined it with marinara as mascara.

Joyce gave her nod of approval to one of her many minions, then snagged Carrie's attention just as she was about to make her escape. "Before you go scrub off and change, could I have a minute please?"

"Sure," Carrie said, quelling an impatient frown. She was ready to come out of the French maid costume and get into her jeans.

"I heard from Jerry today," she said, watching her closely.

Carrie's stomach knotted. Jerry was Philip's producer. "Oh?"

"Philip's come on board. We've got everything in place for the *Summer Sizzling* programming and will kick it off next week. I know it's last minute, but we've pulled together the breakdowns for each show and would like for you and Philip to get together at some point over the weekend and go over them. We'll leave that up to the two of you. The breakdowns are in your dressing room."

Carrie didn't know what was more intimidating— the idea that she'd start this week-long session with Philip or the notion of purposely seeking him out this weekend to make plans for a special she knew he'd been coerced into doing. Her stomach rolled.

Oh, joy.

"You're both professionals. We don't anticipate any problems."

Lucky them, because she sure as hell did. Just because he'd agreed to do the session didn't mean that he was "on board." It merely meant that after months of harassing him and threatening him with God knows what, he'd merely stopped resisting.

Joyce scribbled something on a piece of paper and handed it to her. "Here's Philip's number. If you don't hear from him by noon tomorrow, er…go ahead and give him a call, would you?" She did a perky little nod that was in no way encouraging.

Meaning, he's not going to call you, Carrie thought, feeling the first prickling of irritation along her nerves. "Joyce, are you sure this is a good idea? I mean, he obviously doesn't want to—"

"It'll be fine," Joyce assured her, propelling her off set. "Philip's a good guy. He just likes doing things his own way. Rumor has it he did a similar special with the BBC and it ended badly. This isn't going to end badly. It's a one-week segment to jazz summer ratings. There's no ulterior motive here. Once Philip sees that, he'll be fine."

Now, that was an interesting little tidbit, Carrie thought. She hadn't been privy to that rumor, though she did remember seeing Philip paired up with a busty brunette in some of the reruns she'd run across on one of the British stations which came with her satellite cable package.

Come to think of it, he'd ended his British cable career shortly thereafter and joined the staff here in New Orleans. Had that been why? Carrie wondered now. Did the brunette—the one she'd been envious of—have anything to do with why he'd left London and made the move to New Orleans?

"If you don't mind, when you've nailed things down with him give me a buzz and let me know."

Carrie nodded. "Sure."

Joyce let go a little sigh. "Great. You're a peach."

And he was the pit, Carrie decided uncharitably.

She and Joyce parted ways in the hall, leaving Carrie free to retreat to her room, wash her face and change. The former took much longer than the latter—it didn't take much to removed a nightie and slip into shorts and a tank top—but by the time she'd wiped the last of the lipstick from her mouth, she felt inordinately better.

Or as better as she could feel knowing that the waking nightmare she'd feared was about to become a reality.

And to make matters worse, *she* was going to have to make initial contact because Mr. High and Mighty couldn't be troubled to be so professional. Which really sucked, Carrie thought, growing more agitated by the minute. She attacked the tangles in her hair. Why were men destined to be the bane of her existence?

Honestly, she'd finally got Martin out of her life—had just begun to enjoy a small amount of peace—and now Philip Mallory was in line to screw it up. What had she ever done to him? Why was the idea of hosting a measly week-long special with her so deplorable?

Granted she hadn't been in this business as long as him, but she'd jumped right in and learned the ropes quickly enough. To be honest, Carrie had been watching various food networks/cooking shows for years and had always imagined the hosts having a gravy job. It looked simple enough. Stand in front of a camera and do what you do best, toss a joke in once in a while and voilà!—it was done.

Not so.

Learning to read a teleprompter, knowing which camera to look at, being able to improvise when something didn't work exactly right—that was hard. She'd gone through a grueling month—long training session—in costume, no less—which had involved dealing with broken blenders, lighting problems, garbled teleprompter instructions and missing ingredients. She'd had to learn to be comfortable in front of the camera, because all shows were taped live. Furthermore, a host could never stop a show. Once the cue came from the producer, the game was on and there was no stopping.

But there were perks, as well. For instance, she'd assumed that she'd be responsible for gathering the ingredients, doing her own prep work. The network employed shoppers who took care of finding the best ingredients and the kitchen staff took care of the prep work and *mise en place*—a fancy French term for "in its place" which essentially meant that everything was prepared and ready up to the actual point of cooking.

Admittedly, that was nice. Other than chopping a few things here and there, the majority of the work was done so that she could make the most of her time by teaching their viewers how to prepare the meals she'd chosen.

Furthermore, Carrie had her own sous chef— Jean-Luc, a handsome French godsend who happened to actually admire her skill—who test ran every recipe for the powers-that-be and time constraints. Once it passed muster, all things were a go.

Though the producers had originally wanted her to focus on spicy dishes, Carrie had objected. She enjoyed preparing all different kinds of meals and didn't want to be limited to "hot" fare simply to enhance a marketing hook.

Even packaged as a Playboy centerfold, her skill was their hook thank you very much.

Though she'd had serious reservations, she'd agreed to be their *Negligee Gourmet,* but she'd had no intention of compromising on the food. That was a hill she'd been prepared to die on and, thanks to the agent Tate Hatcher—Zora's husband—had recommended, she'd ultimately gotten her way.

Carrie briefly entertained the idea of contacting her agent about this and seeing if perhaps she could do anything. Nancy Rutherford was a rottweiler in toy poodle's clothing. On the surface she was delicate and sweet, but when it came time to negotiate she could tear up a contract with the best of them.

Regardless, it was a little late in the game to object now, particularly when she'd already given her consent. If she bailed now, she'd only make herself look bad and, unlike Philip, she had less experience in the business and therefore more to lose. If she had any prayer of at some point hosting a show in something more than a half-yard of fabric she couldn't afford to risk a reputation of being difficult to work with.

Carrie braided her hair and secured it with a band. Better to make the best of it and move on. She'd endured four years with Martin. Surely to God she could handle one week with Philip Mallory. She stuffed the breakdowns into her purse and her lips formed a ghost of a smile.

If nothing else, he was easier to look at.

In perfect punctuation of that thought, she pulled open her dressing-room door and drew up short at the sight of Philip's startled look.

Carrie blinked, stunned. Her entire body tingled from the soles of her feet to the top of her head. Her breath disturbingly vanished from her lungs and her heart threatened to gallop right out of her chest. You know, she'd realized he was tall, but she'd never truly appreciated just how tall he really was until he was standing less than two feet from her.

He cocked his head and a tentative smile caught the corner of his sexy mouth. "Er...sorry. I was looking for Carrie Robbins."

Oh, now this was fun, Carrie thought, struggling to bring her unruly body back under control. He didn't recognize her without the makeup. She managed a grin. "You've found her."

His eyes widened and a gratifying blush stained his cheeks. "I—" He paused, seemingly at a loss, and looked her up and down. "Sorry. I, uh... I didn't recognize you."

"I'm wearing clothes," Carrie replied dryly. "It tends to throw people."

"Quite right," he said distractedly. "I'm sure I would have recognized your breasts."

Carrie made a little choking noise, something between a gasp and a chuckle. She didn't know whether to be insulted or flattered.

"Bugger," Philip swore. "Did I say that aloud? I said that aloud, didn't I? Sorry," he apologized sheepishly. "I'm Philip Mallory, by the way."

Trying very hard not to be charmed by the whole distractedly adorable British shtick, Carrie smiled. "I know who you are."

"Oh, good. Then we're both on the same page." His gaze lingered over her face once more, still seemingly shocked to discover that she looked normal beneath the paint. "So," he said, clearing his throat. "I assume your producer has mentioned the *Summer Sizzling* special to you?"

"She has. Just a few minutes ago, in fact."

"Excellent. And you got the breakdowns?"

She nodded. "I did."

"Jerry mentioned that we should get together over the weekend. Is there any particular time that would work best for you?"

So he'd had the balls to seek her out *and* was deferring to her schedule as well? For someone who'd been dead set against the idea, he was certainly coming around swiftly enough. Almost too swiftly, Carrie thought suspiciously.

"I'm free tomorrow night if that'll work for you," she said, pettily hoping to ruin any dating plans he might have had.

Philip nodded without hesitation. "That's fine. Perhaps a working dinner, then?"

"Sure. Mama Mojo's, sixish?"

"That suits me." He paused, pushed a hand through his hair, shot her another curious look. "Well, I won't keep you. I'll, er… See you tomorrow night."

"Right," Carrie said, totally unnerved by the unexpected, bizarre encounter as she watched him walk away. Her gaze lingered over those loose dark auburn curls at the nape of his neck, the broad scope of shoulders, followed his spine, then settled predictably on his ass.

Encased in a pair of worn denim jeans which were loose enough for comfort, but tight enough to give her imagination a break, he looked sexy as hell. She mentally removed the jeans and entertained the truffle oil fantasy again. Warmth burned the tops of her thighs and a thin breath seeped past her curiously dry lips.

Oh, hell, she thought with a resigned sigh. Time

to buy those combat boots. Or, judging by her exaggerated reaction to him, maybe full body armor was more in order.

2

I WOULD HAVE RECOGNIZED your breasts? Philip thought, cheeks burning with uncustomary heat as he made his way to his car. In other words, he'd spent so much time looking at her breasts that he didn't recognize her face?

What a freaking nightmare.

She had to think he was a lecherous idiot.

Things had definitely not gone according to plan, that was for damned sure, he thought with a grunt of disgust. Within minutes of Rupert making the call to let the execs know he was on board, he'd gotten a relieved call from Jerry. Things would be fine. Just a special to boost summer ratings. There was no plan to hijack his show or permanently pair him up with Carrie. No worries. Seriously. Thanks for being a team player.

Mostly the same spiel they'd given Rupert, but something about it coming from Jerry made him feel marginally better about the whole thing. He'd certainly never gotten any such assurance from his previous producer, that was for damned sure. But that didn't mean he planned to let his guard down, though. It just meant that, for the time being, everything appeared kosher.

Furthermore, though he'd come on board, it was obvious that they didn't expect his complete cooperation. Jerry had offered to courier the breakdowns in order to save Philip a trip back down to the studio—save him all of thirty minutes—then had gone on to say that he and Carrie would need to get together over the weekend to familiarize themselves with the new format, but that she'd contact him. Not to put himself out.

The rumor of his unwillingness to commit to the special had been buzzing around the network for months—she had to know that he didn't want to do it. Most likely she'd heard why, too, so he had no intention of apologizing for it. He'd watched her often enough to know that she was smart—she could put the pieces together. But what she didn't know was that if this had to happen, *he* was going to be in charge.

Meaning *he* intended to run the show.

So there'd been none of this she'll-get-in-touch-with-you crap. He'd planned to make the first move, set the tone for the next of week. He would lead, she would follow, and either she could fall in line and do things the way he wanted to, or she'd be miserable. It was as simple as that. A hard-assed approach, but it was better than losing his show.

Again.

Unfortunately, he'd lost the upper hand the instant she'd opened her dressing-room door and everything had gone depressingly downhill from there. He'd been struck dumb and mesmerized and, as bizarre as it seemed, he'd gotten the strangest inkling that he'd met her before, a sense of *knowing her* that didn't—couldn't—exist. No doubt a result of watching her show, Philip thought absently.

Furthermore, as unbelievable as it was, he'd never seen her out of her *Negligee* costume. In keeping with her show's concept, she was always tramped up like a centerfold. Big hair, little outfits, lots of make-up. A wet dream come to life. Every man's fantasy.

Unequivocally hot.

So who would have ever thought that she'd be even more beautiful *out* of costume? That those indigo eyes which sparkled amid false lashes and mascara would be all the more clear and gorgeous without them? Like sugared violets, Philip thought, then drew up short and snorted.

Christ, he was turning into a bloody poet.

The long and short of it was, she was the most

spectacularly beautiful woman he'd ever seen. Delicate bone structure, a flawless cameo complexion, plump kissable lips and long straight hair the color of moonbeams. No doubt other men had rhapsodized her angelic appearance—and admittedly she had an ethereal look—but Philip couldn't imagine anything on the other side of heaven any more gorgeous than her.

Carrie was…indescribably appealing. Fascinatingly sensual, he thought broodingly.

Furthermore, he'd detected a depth of character that he imagined many men missed. She was smart, quick and funny. Factor in sexy, gorgeous and talented and she became positively lethal.

But she wouldn't be lethal for him, dammit, despite evidence to the contrary. Namely their first encounter.

Philip had planned on citing the time and place for their working dinner, but had been knocked off his game the instant she opened the door. He chuckled darkly. And only by the grace of God had he not been knocked on his ass.

He couldn't afford for that to happen again.

From here on out he was going to be Mr. Professional. In charge and on top of the play. He darted out of the parking garage and into afternoon traffic.

No more fantasizing about bending her over the

counter, or staring at her breasts, or wondering what sort of sexual havoc that hot mouth of hers could wreak upon his body. No more dreams of crowning her breasts with clotted cream and strawberry jam, then lazily licking it off. Of filling her belly button and the twin dimples in the small of her back with warmed chocolate and spooning it out with his tongue. No more dreams of feasting on her until her skin dewed, her sex wept and she cried his name.

Philip's dick jerked against his zipper, forcing a mangled curse from between his lips. A futile bark of laughter erupted from his throat. He could no-more this and no-more that from now until Dooms-day, but it wasn't going to change the fact that he wanted her. Had wanted her from the first instant he'd seen her sashay across her set and pick up a spatula.

But that was the point right? How could he not think about shagging her when she was dressed like that? Which was the height of irony because he found the whole idea of her costume appalling attire for the kitchen. In his opinion it was a cheap mar-keting ploy that devalued her and her skill.

Furthermore, he'd watched enough of her shows to realize that she wasn't altogether comfortable playing the vixen. Oh, she could do it well enough, Philip thought, his lips sliding into a smile. Quite well, in fact. But every once in a while he'd catch a glimpse of strain and instinctively knew it was a direct result of the get-up.

She was a fantastic chef, an excellent host with true star potential. What on earth had possessed her to agree to be *The Negligee Gourmet* when she clearly would rather the show be about the food? The art of pulling a meal together?

Certainly the money was better. He knew that. But for whatever reason—possibly even wishful thinking—he didn't believe it was about the money for Carrie. She simply didn't seem the type. Hell, who knew? Perhaps she merely hoped to parlay the *Negligee* career into a better deal at a later time, but if that was the case, Philip grimly imagined she'd be in for an unpleasant surprise.

Her show had been a huge hit and the execs who were currently patting themselves on the back for their good fortune wouldn't think kindly upon changing the format later. Chances were she'd pigeon-holed herself right into a career he wasn't altogether certain she'd wanted.

But then, what did he know? He'd merely watched her on television and, though the camera was adept at picking up hidden facets of a person's personality, he really didn't know her—he merely thought he did.

And that, my friends, was the beauty of television, Philip thought.

Though he'd rather let hungry buzzards feast upon his privates than do this special with her, Philip couldn't deny that he was keenly interested in discovering what made her tick. He might not like the concept of her show, but peep show aside, he sure as hell loved watching her cook. She was a natural in the kitchen, possessed an innate sense of how to marry flavors and compliment a palate. The kind of talent that had been bestowed at birth, not learned, which made her all the more intriguing.

And, Philip thought with a shaky sigh, he was meeting this walking mystery at Mama Mojo's at six tomorrow night. Ostensibly to put her in her place. Which should be a cool trick considering he was more interested in putting her on her back.

And on her belly.

And on a table.

And against a wall.

Really, the possibilities were endless.

"OKAY," FRANKIE SALVATERRA announced above the din at the Blue Monkey pub in the famed French Quarter. "It's time to officially call the Bitch-Fest to order." Her gaze darted around the table. "Who wants to go first?"

One of the perks to having a day job was never missing or being late for their standing Friday-night pastime—the Bitch-Fest. God knows it had gotten Carrie though many a trying time. Something about sharing her angst among her fellow CHiC friends— Zora, Frankie and April—had made her problems seem a lot lighter. And with good reason—when she shared them, they were divided.

"No takers?" Frankie said when no one immediately responded. "Fine. I'll go first." She paused, scanned the faces which held her attention. "I'm tired of being engaged," she said matter-of-factly. "I want to get married. Now."

"Now?" Zora parroted, seemingly stunned. "But there's no way your planner can pull together the ceremony that you and Ross have outlined *now*. It's physically impossible."

Frankie and Ross's wedding plans had begun to rival that of Charles and Diana's. She'd commissioned doves, ice sculptures, rare orchids and had hired a local coveted designer—Madame LeBeau, who was rumored to be positively impossible to work with—to do both her dress and the bridesmaids' ensembles.

April Wilson-Hayes sipped her margarita. "She's right. Logistically, it's just not possible."

"I know that," Frankie replied archly. "Which is

why we're culling all of those plans and starting over."

Every woman seated at their table with the exception of Frankie groaned at this pronouncement.

Zora, however, was the first to offer an opinion and predictably, it wasn't sugar-coated. "That's insane," she said, absently rubbing a hand over her very pregnant belly. "You've spent a fortune pulling the 'wedding of your dreams' together. You wanted something grand and feminine and beautiful."

No doubt to counteract some of the lingering insecurities wrought by her father, Carrie thought sadly. Geez, that horrible old bastard had really done a number on her. Fortunately she'd met a guy who knew that—knew what she needed—and loved her enough to indulge her.

"What do you mean you're starting over?" Zora continued, still evidently outraged.

"You know," Frankie said, "I was really expecting a little bit of support here." Looking distinctly sly, she dunked the lime floating in her club soda.

Club soda? Carrie thought, squinting thoughtfully. Now that was odd. She'd known Frankie Salvaterra for almost ten years and she'd never seen her drink a club soda. Particularly in a bar. Carrie inwardly gasped, shot her friend a closer look.

Frankie's lips twitched with a barely suppressed

grin. "We're starting over because if I don't get married now, I'm not going to fit in my dress."

April frowned. "Not going to fit in your—"

Zora looked from Frankie's drink to her smug smile and inhaled sharply. "You're pregnant!" she breathed, eyes twinkling with unabashed joy.

Frankie beamed and nodded. "I am," she confirmed proudly.

April squealed, Carrie laughed, and Zora positively glowed. "Oh, Frankie," she said, taking her friend's hand. "You're going to make the best mama."

Frankie dabbed at her eyes and smiled. "And you guys are going to make the best honorary aunts." She swallowed, took a deep breath and appeared to be attempting to gather her wits. "So here's the deal. We want to get married next weekend—Saturday—and I need your help. We're paring down the guest list from fifteen hundred to fifteen. The people who are important to me are the ones we see on a regular basis. To hell with all the others," she said with a dismissive wave of her hand. "They're only showing up for the food."

Speaking of which, Carrie thought. "I'll cater," she promptly volunteered. "It'll be my gift."

"And I know the perfect place," April said. She

tucked her hair behind her ears. "You can have Ben's and my tree."

The tree in question was a two-hundred-plus-year-old live oak which had held special meaning for them. They'd originally planned to host their own wedding there beneath its sheltering branches, but the timing had been off. Too cold. New Orleans summer heat was notorious, but the shade of that tree would undoubtedly end up being just as cool as a crowded reception room.

"Oh, April," Frankie said, choking up. "I think that would be perfect."

"And we'll designate Ben as the photographer," she added, then chuckled. "You can bet he'll have a camera with him anyway."

"Then all that leaves is the honeymoon," Zora told her. "And Tate and I would like to have that honor."

"Zora," Frankie gasped softly. "That's too much."

"I insist," she said. Which was the last word. When Zora made up her mind, that was it. Conversation over.

Frankie's dark brown eyes glittered with liquid emotion and her face softened with untold joy. "I knew I could count on you guys."

Zora reached over and squeezed her hand again.

"Always." She let go a breath. "Now who wants to bitch next?"

April shook her head, shot them all a contented smile. "Sorry. I got nothing."

And no wonder, Carrie thought. After more than a decade apart, April had been reunited with her special someone, her soul mate, Ben. She had every reason to be happy.

"Stop bragging," Carrie finally teased. She rolled her eyes. "Sheesh, you happy people are nauseating. All pregnant and in love."

Zora turned to Frankie. "Has the nausea started yet?" she wanted to know. "Because if it has I can tell you that eating a saltine cracker before I get out of bed and having Tate rub my feet helps considerably."

"What does rubbing your feet have to do with being nauseated?" April asked.

Zora pulled a negligent shrug and smiled coyly. "Nothing. It just makes me feel better."

Carrie chuckled. "Very devious. I like it."

Zora cast her a considering look. "So if our happiness is making you nauseated, does that mean that something's happened that's made you *un*happy?"

Shrewd as always, Carrie thought, swirling her straw around her drink.

"It's the Brit, isn't it?" Frankie said. "The hot one with the great ass?"

Carrie felt a grin tug at her lips. Frankie certainly had a way of cutting straight to the heart of the matter. "That would be the one, yes."

"Ah… Let me guess," April chimed in. "The special has finally come through."

Carrie let go a sigh and nodded. "We start next week."

"Next week?" Frankie asked shrilly. "When did you hear about this?"

"Today."

"Good grief," April moaned, appalled. "How do they expect the two of you to be ready in that kind of time frame?"

"We're 'professionals,'" Carrie quoted. "And we're meeting at Mama Mojo's at six tomorrow night to go over the breakdowns and new format."

Zora quirked a disbelieving brow. "You mean to tell me that they expect you to be ready to do this on Monday?"

"They do," Carrie confirmed.

"Can you?" April asked, the most practical of the bunch. "I mean, is it possible?"

Carrie cocked her head and smiled sadly. "I guess it has to be."

"This is outrageous," Zora said. "Did you call Nancy?"

"There's no point," Carrie told her. "I agreed to it months ago."

She frowned, cocked her head and a lock of red hair slid from behind her ear. "But I don't understand. What's been the hold up? Why are you just getting started now?"

Carrie's lips quirked with bitter humor. "My future cohost has been the holdout. I don't know whether he takes exception to me or my show, but suffice it to say he's been vehemently opposed to doing the special with me."

"Sounds like an uninformed bastard," Frankie said, gratifyingly annoyed on Carrie's behalf.

April paused consideringly. "I don't know," she said. "I watch his show. I wouldn't have expected this out of him."

Her either, Carrie thought, heartened by the fact that she hadn't been the only one who'd misjudged his character. She shared the rumor she'd gotten from Joyce this afternoon regarding the special gone bad with the BBC.

"Now that makes more sense," Zora said. "You're smart, funny and beautiful and, more importantly, you are damned fine at what you do. If he has a problem hosting a show with you, I really find it hard to believe that it's personal. I'd be willing to bet he's got his own reasons and they have nothing to do with you."

She hoped Zora was right. It would certainly make the next week easier to get through, that was for sure. At any rate, she knew that a small part of it was personal. When she'd called Joyce this afternoon to confirm the rendezvous with Philip, her producer had shared another interesting tidbit.

Carrie felt a smile tug at her lips. "I do know that he's asked the producers if we can tone down the 'centerfold' image while we're working together."

Frankie chuckled. "Probably afraid he'll inadvertently close his pecker in the oven." She nodded and those dark brown eyes flickered with intelligence. "Now we're getting to the heart of the matter. Mr. Stuffy Brit obviously has the hots for you."

Carrie's heart did an odd little flutter. She shook her head. "I don't think so."

April and Zora shared a look. "I don't know, Carrie," April said. "That's a pretty telling request. Clearly he's worried about staying focused."

Carrie took a sip of her drink and shifted in her seat. "I think he's more worried about tainting himself with my lesser moral standards."

Frankie let go an exasperated sigh. "For the last

time, Carrie, you have not sold out! I know you'll be happier when you can negotiate a better deal—"

"You mean when I can wear clothes," she said.

"—but in the meantime, you're just upping your value. You've got a helluva following."

"But will they follow me when I'm not painted up like a streetwalker?" she asked quietly. Carrie admitted another niggling fear. "I, uh…" She pushed her hair away from her face. "I think that instead of upping my value, I may have marketed myself right out of a normal hosting position. You know what they say," she said, pulling a shrug. "If it ain't broke, don't fix it. When it comes time to renew my contract, what's going to make them let me have my way? What's going to motivate them?"

"Your talent," Zora said simply. "Because at the heart of your show, that's what it's all about." She smiled softly. "We watch you, Carrie. You're passionate about what you do and you're good at it. Granted some viewers might be watching to see if your boobs fall out of your nightie, but the majority of your audience simply enjoys spending a half hour with you."

Carefully hopeful, Carrie sighed. "I hope you're right."

Zora nodded imperiously. "I know I am. Just wait and see."

Frankie smiled wickedly. "In the meantime, I think you need to torture him. He wants you to wear something different—fine," she said with a devious nod. "If I were you, I'd wear *less.*"

Carrie chuckled. "I don't know that it's possible."

"Oh, it is," April said, getting into the spirit of Frankie's revenge. "Frankie's right. He's held out and hurt your feelings—"

Startled, Carrie looked up. "No, he—"

"Yes, he has and there's no point in denying it. You've watched him for years. I've heard you talk about him before, and when this thing at *Let's Cook, New Orleans!* came through, you couldn't wait to meet him."

All true, Carrie knew.

"Furthermore," Frankie chimed in, "we all know that you've had a crush on him."

Carrie started to deny it, but a firm look from Frankie made her change her mind.

"You have," she insisted. "You, my dear friend, have been presented with a perfect opportunity. One week, a hot co-host who needs an attitude adjustment, and the opportunity to start cooking with something other than gas."

Carrie couldn't help it, she chuckled and shook her head. "You're crazy."

"And you haven't been laid in months."

Closer to a year, but she wasn't going to admit that. Between the hours she'd worked for Martin, then starting the new show, things had been too crazy to pursue romance of any kind. But a relationship with Philip? When she suspected what he thought of her?

Not no, but hell no.

Zora studied her carefully. "Even if you're not in the market for romance, I think a little calculated retribution is in order." She cocked her head and smiled. "And now that you know his weakness… Well," she said. "It's up to you, of course."

Carrie merely smiled. She wasn't so much worried about his weaknesses as her own. It would be heartily embarrassing to set out to teach him a lesson and end up not making the grade herself.

Or worse, God forbid, falling for him.

3

AT PRECISELY FOUR MINUTES after six, Philip covertly watched Carrie weave her way through the throng of tables to the one he'd been shown to in the back. Though she appeared completely oblivious to the attention her entrance garnered, he knew she couldn't be. Heads turned as she walked past. Flickering looks of interest from men—envy from women—followed her as she cut a path through the crowded restaurant.

How did she stand it? Philip wondered absently. That constant attention? It had to be bloody nerve-racking.

Wearing a cool pale yellow sheath dress, long hair hanging like a silvery-blonde curtain down her back, and a pair of strappy sandals on her feet, Carrie looked classically gorgeous. Her face was scrubbed clean of makeup—in fact, the tip of her nose had that squeaky clean glow—odd that he should find that adorable—and other than being naturally sexy, no traces of her *Negligee* persona were evident.

Once again he was struck by the difference. The change was unbelievably dramatic, the perfectly rare combination of wholesome and sexy. For reasons he couldn't explain, his breath quickened, his palms grew clammy and a line of gooseflesh raced up his back. He'd experienced these unwanted symptoms before when he'd watched her show, but seeing her in the flesh compounded them significantly.

He stood—to his chagrin, somewhat shakily— when she neared their table. "Is this spot all right?" he asked. "It was the closest thing to private available."

Carrie nodded, seated herself in the chair he'd pulled out for her. "Sure. I hope I haven't kept you waiting long."

"No," he said. "I've, uh… I've only been here a few minutes. Just long enough to peruse the menu."

She looked up and her violet gaze tangled with his, causing a curious whirling sensation behind his navel. "You've never been here before?"

Trying hard not to be mesmerized, Philip shook his head. "Er…no. I can't say that I've enjoyed the pleasure."

Her lips formed an enchanting smile. "Oh, then

you're in for a treat. Personally, I always have the jambalaya. It's some of the best in the area."

"I'll take your recommendation then," Philip told her, offering her a smile. Best to soften her up with pleasantries before he proceeded with the mandates, he decided. Provided he'd even remember them. Once again he could feel his brain turning to mush and his dick thickening in her glowing presence.

Thankfully once the waiter had supplied drinks and taken their order, he'd regained a modicum of his composure. "Have you had a chance to look at the breakdowns yet?" he asked.

Carrie nodded, bent down and withdrew them from her purse. "I have. I noticed in keeping with the 'sizzling' theme, there are several spicy dishes. Are there any that you object to? Anything you want to tweak or change?"

"No," Philip said. He paused, blew out a breath. "Look, before we go any further, do you mind if I'm completely honest with you, Carrie?"

The smallest hint of a smile tugged at the corner of her lips. "Who wouldn't prefer the truth to a lie?"

Philip hesitated. He'd been rehearsing this spiel for the past couple of hours and yet now that the time had come to make good his delivery, he was having a hard time keeping to the diplomatic but hard-assed approach. He leaned forward. "I'm sure that you've heard that I wasn't particularly keen to do this special."

Her eyes sparkled with wry humor. "I might have heard mention of it once or twice."

Again that charming humor, he thought. "Did you happen to hear mention of why?"

The bane of his recent existence calmly sipped her drink and pulled a light shrug. "Just an unconfirmed rumor."

"Well, let me give you the official version. The last time I did a 'special' my female co-host hijacked my show." His voice inexplicably hardened. "Don't take it personally, but I have no intention of letting that happen again."

The faintest hint of irritation tightened her otherwise serene features.

"I'm the one with the most experience here," he continued, "and if it's all the same to you, rather than being equal partners per se, I'd prefer that you think of yourself as an assistant."

Her compelling eyes widened fractionally. "An assistant?" she repeated tightly.

"Sort of like my Vanna White," Philip said, giving her an analogy he hoped she'd understand. He'd grown quite fond of *The Wheel of Fortune* since moving to New Orleans. Fascinating game, really.

"I'm not a letter-turner on a game show—I'm a

chef," Carrie said, her smooth voice slightly strangled with what Philip belatedly realized was anger.
"As for being your assistant, if it's all the same to
you," she said, patronizingly throwing his phrasing
back at him, "*I'd* just as soon stick to the format."

Philip winced. Frankly, he hadn't really expected
her to argue with him. His was the voice of experience after all. But he could tell by the somewhat
mulish set of her jaw and the white circle around her
supremely sexy mouth that she was heartily displeased. What? he wondered. Did she not like
Vanna?

"I've insulted you," he said.

"Now that's insightful," she replied sarcastically.

Hmm, Philip thought with a mental wince. That
was bad...because he really hadn't gotten to the part
where he'd assumed he'd offend her. But there was
no way around it, and he was a firm believer in
speaking his mind. Fewer misunderstandings that
way. Besides, after the Sophie debacle he didn't appreciate subterfuge.

"I won't argue the point that you're a chef, and a
damned fine one to boot," he said. "I've watched
your show, have even eaten at Chez Martin's several
times before you joined the network. It's not your
ability that I'm concerned with," he told her. He
leaned back in his seat and regarded her moodily.

"Frankly, it's your attire. I've asked the producers to let you wear clothes during our special, but they've said no." His lips quirked. "Evidently your audience expects you to be naked," he drawled.

Carrie's mouth formed a smile that lacked warmth. "I'm *not* naked," she said, her voice cracking with barely suppressed anger. "I'm merely… scantily clad."

Philip smiled blandly. "Well, for all intents and purposes, you might as well be."

Her eyes narrowed. "But I'm *not*."

"Look," he said. "It's a cooking show, not soft porn. You look quite fetching in your little gowns and such, I'll admit—"

Vast understatement. His penis all but exploded every time he got a glimpse of her barely covered ass.

"—but those outfits are better suited to a bedroom than a kitchen, particularly one that broadcasts into thousands of homes. It undermines the work. Myself personally, I'd prefer things more about the food and less about your breasts."

A beat slid into five. He watched her struggle with the effort to maintain composure, but ultimately she managed to rein in her temper. More's the pity, Philip thought, slightly disappointed. He'd love to tangle with her.

"Were it up to me, I would like the same," she replied tightly. "But as it's not up to you or me, I think we might as well accept things as they are and move on."

So it was as he suspected, Philip thought, immeasurably pleased. Being their *Negligee Gourmet* wasn't her ultimate goal. "I wish it were that simple."

"We both signed contracts," she snapped impatiently. "It has to be. And for the record," she continued, "I'm not interested in hijacking your show because, unlike your last co-host, I already have one."

"But not one where you get to wear clothes," he pointed out, needling her. He enjoyed another drink of wine. "I suspect you'd like one without a gimmick—again, like mine—and, just so we're clear, *mine's* not available."

She leaned forward and pinned him with a surprisingly hard stare. "And just so we're clear, *I don't want it.*"

So she says now, Philip thought. But should the opportunity present itself, she'd undoubtedly take it. In his experience—case in point, Sophie—women were like that.

He smiled, continued to study her, then ultimately decided to let it drop. He'd annoyed her enough this evening and, if nothing else, had proven his point.

"Then we shouldn't have any problem. What say we check out those breakdowns, shall we?"

HE HAD TO BE THE MOST insufferably irritating man she'd ever had the misfortune to share a meal with, Carrie thought as she all but stomped into the ladies' room. Nature hadn't called, but if she'd sat there a moment longer she wasn't altogether sure she could have held her temper. Even Martin-the-provoking-bastard hadn't successfully angered her past her boiling point, but something about Philip Mallory's almost-but-not-quite condescending high-brow tone made her twitch and seethe with irritation.

While she was routinely guilty of seething, she'd never given anyone the power to provoke her into twitching. The fact that Philip had managed to do it five minutes into their first effort at working together told her two things.

One, he was a bastard, albeit a sexy one.

And, two, he was a sexy bastard who could easily get under her skin.

Because, strangely enough, much as she loathed to admit it, she'd found the whole exchange quite...titillating. She'd been practically mesmerized by the same sexy mouth he'd been gleefully insulting her with.

It wasn't fair, Carrie thought, to pair such a beautiful set of lips with such an undeserving recipient. Were there any justice in the world, he'd have the thin, bloodless altogether unappealing lips of a bottom-feeder. They'd certainly complement his character, she thought uncharitably.

As it was, he had the most intriguing mouth she'd ever seen. His lips were slightly full, his smile a bit crooked and the promise to sin lurked in that sensually wicked curve. To make matters worse, she instinctively knew he'd taste like all of the above—hot, thrilling, wicked and sexy.

Carrie braced both hands on the vanity, stared at her reflection in the mirror and let go a disgusted breath.

And she also knew that if she didn't watch herself, she'd be gravitating toward that mouth like a devoted familiar, unable to think for herself. A mindless handmaiden, beholden to the devil himself.

Lucky for her she didn't have any intention of letting anything like that happen. He may be one of the best-looking men she'd ever seen—all right, probably *the best*—and she wasn't in the habit of lying to herself, so she could admit that she'd been—and to her eternal mortification still was—incredibly attracted to him.

But that was before she'd been subjected to his pithy commentary on her *Negligee* attire. That was before the arrogant blockhead had tried to demote her to an "assistant." Of all the freakin' nerve. Who the hell did he think he was? Now she knew why he'd shown up at her dressing-room door the instant things had been declared a go—he'd wanted to take charge.

Ha!

Like hell.

Evidently—depressingly—Philip Mallory had made the same mistake lots of men had made about her—he'd underestimated her. *She's pretty. She's stacked. Surely if God blessed her with good looks, she's lacking good sense. She can't possibly be smart, can she?*

Carrie smiled humorlessly. It had been that way since her late teens. Evidently most men thought her brain had migrated to her breasts the instant she'd had enough to fill a C-cup. To know that Philip seemed to fit into that category was a lot more depressing than it should have been. After all, she was used to it. So used to it in fact that she rarely thought enough of a guy to *let* him disappoint her.

That he'd managed to warrant enough emotion to let her down when she barely knew him told her that if she didn't get things under control pretty damned quick, she was going to be in trouble. Clearly the charming guy who'd been welcomed—and often anxiously awaited—into her living room via the television set for the past couple of years was simply a character he played, and the sooner she learned the difference, the better off she'd be. Carrie sighed, swallowed her disappointment.

If only the TV had lied about how fantastically good-looking—translate: *sexy, magnetic, compelling, beautiful, etc.*—he was, she'd be fine.

Honestly, the man just did something for her. That wavy dark auburn hair, the way it curled at the nape of his neck. Those intelligent, heavy-lidded silver eyes, the perfect combination of clever and broodingly sexy. The shape of his jaw, the angle of his cheek and that slightly crooked smile… All of it combined was enough to make her breath seep out in a sigh, her heart leap and her sex burn.

And under present circumstances, that was a recipe for disaster.

Besides, after the way he'd acted this evening, she'd decided to dish up a little retribution. When Carrie had walked into this restaurant tonight she'd had every intention of being professional and courteous—even knowing that he hadn't wanted to do the special with her, so frankly, she thought she was being quite nice about the whole thing. The idea of taking her friends' advice—of upping the sex factor of her performance and wearing less simply to distract him—had been completely out of the question.

Until five minutes ago.

Clearly Philip Mallory needed a lesson in humility and she wasn't a founding member of Chicks in Charge for nothing. When pushed far enough, she'd push back and, curiously, the idea of figuratively knocking Philip on his delectable British ass was vastly appealing.

She couldn't fault him for wanting the show to be more about the food and less about her breasts—she did, too—but trying to patronizingly bully her into being his assistant because he disapproved set her teeth on edge. The only thing he needed to concern himself with was how well she did her job—a job she was quite good at, dammit. Instead, he'd stepped over the line and thereby pushed her over hers.

He would regret it, Carrie thought as a slow smile slid around her lips. For the first time in her life she was actually looking forward to taking advantage of her sex appeal.

Carrie had enough experience with the opposite sex to know when a guy was attracted to her and, while Philip Mallory might not want to feel the chemistry between them, she knew he did. Frankie had been right. He'd spent entirely too much time staring at her mouth to indicate otherwise. She'd felt that keen lazy gaze trail over her lips, down her neck—even on those breasts which had been such a hot topic of conversation. No doubt it galled him, too, Carrie thought, but in the end it wouldn't matter.

He'd gotten the wrong tiger by the tail this time.

Heartened by her plan, Carrie freshened her lip-gloss, then exited the bathroom. She was halfway across the dining room when she noticed that some-one—a distinctly *female* someone—had taken her seat and that Philip had gone on the charm offensive, smiling and talking as though he didn't have a care in the world.

As though she weren't here.

Irritation stiffened her spine and she was caught off guard by an unexpected simultaneous burst of envy and jealousy. Neither of which she cared for. A telling sentiment lurked in that realization, but she deliberately pushed it aside and summoned a forced smile as she neared their table.

"…and that's the trick to it," Philip said amiably. "Coat your spatula with a shot of nonstick spray and you won't have any problem turning your omelet next time, I assure you."

"That's all there is to it?" the groupie in her seat gushed as though Philip had just given her the power to end world hunger. "Really?"

"Really," Carrie inserted with a brittle smile. Philip's gaze had slid to her, a silent acknowledgement, but he'd continued to politely bask in the glow of what was clearly a fan's enthusiasm.

The woman's startled gaze swung to Carrie. A flicker of instant dislike dimmed her starstruck gaze as she swiftly sized her up. "Er…we're talking," she said, doing a little hand motion between herself and Philip that indicated Carrie wasn't welcome. "Do you mind?"

Resisting the impulse to drag her up by the hair of her head, Carrie gritted her teeth. "I mind that you're in my chair."

She blinked as though she didn't quite understand. Evidently too stupid, Carrie thought, growing increasingly annoyed. Philip, damn him, looked on with smug humor.

"Forgive me, Beth, for being so rude," Philip belatedly chimed in. "This is my assistant, Carrie Robbins."

Carrie shot him a withering look. *"Coworker,"* she corrected.

"We're having a working dinner," he explained.

"Yes," Carrie added. "And we're not finished yet. I'd like dessert." She looked pointedly at Beth. "My chair?"

Looking extremely disgruntled, Beth finally removed her sizable ass from Carrie's chair. She pulled a smile together for Philip's benefit. "It was a pleasure to meet you. Like I said, I, uh—" she bent and awkwardly gathered her purse "—I watch you all the time."

Philip beamed at her, the wretch. "Thank you."

Carrie received a considerably less warm smile—slightly sick, in fact—as she walked away.

Philip relaxed against his chair and absently scratched his chest. "Charming girl," he said. "Had a spatula problem."

"Thank God you could help her," Carrie remarked drolly.

His lips quirked. "You're mad again," he tutted infuriatingly. He shot her a questioning glance. "You don't have some sort of anger management problem I should know about, do you?"

"No," Carrie said. "Ordinarily I'm pretty unflappable."

His gaze seemed to sharpen with interest. "Meaning I'm the problem?" he asked innocently. "Perhaps you should go back and tell Joyce that I'm too much bother and that you can't possibly work with me."

She knew that was his game, but she hadn't expected him to tip his hand quite so quickly. Carrie struggled to suppress a smile and shook her head. "That pesky contract," she reminded him.

He grimaced. "Yeah. Personally, I thought my agent had taken care of that little niggling detail this time."

From the tone of his voice, his agent had probably come damned close to strangulation when Philip had learned that he hadn't, Carrie thought.

He threw back the rest of his drink. "Clearly I'm going to have to pay better attention the next time negotiations come 'round." He gave her a thoughtful look. "And you should, too." He scowled adorably. "In fact, you should fire your agent altogether and get a new one, then you might actually be able to wear something that doesn't scream 'I'll shag you!' during your show." His displeased expression increased. "Week before last you came dangerously close to setting that fur trim attached to your bodice on fire. Ridiculous," he muttered. "Bloody ridiculous."

"I have no intention of firing my agent," Carrie told him, inordinately heartened by the fact that he'd watched her often enough to note a potential mishap. Still, she thought as she struggled to flatten a smile, the man was insufferable. "Is there an opinion you have that you *don't* share?" she asked.

"No," he told her moodily. "It's part of my charm."

She smiled sweetly. "Did your agent tell you that?"

Philip laughed, a soft sexy chuckle that made the fine hairs on her arms stand on end and, for the briefest of moments, she got a glimpse of the guy she'd always thought he'd been, the one her foolish heart thought it recognized. She let go a shaky sigh.

"Touché," he said softly.

"Is there anything else we need to go over?" she asked, suddenly ready to call an end to this encounter. She could deal with smart-ass Philip a whole lot better than the guy she'd hoped he'd be. That guy was dangerous.

Philip sighed heavily. "If you're going to adhere to your principles and not renege on your contract, then no, I suppose not." His silvery gaze slid to hers causing her breath to hitch in her throat. "But I thought you wanted dessert."

Carrie snagged enough cash to cover her meal and a tip from her wallet and put it in the middle of the table. "Mine's waiting at home."

He arched a surprised brow. "I thought you were single."

"I am."

His eyes widened significantly as he gratifyingly jumped to the wrong conclusion, that she had a guy at home. "Well, then."

Carrie knew she should tell him that the only thing waiting at home for her was Hoover, her dog—so named for his tendency to eat anything he found on the floor whether it be trash or food—and a lovely carton of Godiva ice cream.

She knew she should…but in the end, she didn't. Let him wonder, Carrie thought. A petty form of retribution, but she'd take it where she could.

She smiled, slung her purse over her shoulder. "See you Monday," she said.

Seemingly resigned, he tossed some bills on the table as well and stood when she did. "Yes, but I daresay I'll be seeing *a lot* more of you."

Carrie chuckled softly at his miserable tone. If he only knew, she thought. If he only knew…

4

"I HAD PLANS, YOU KNOW," Rupert announced testily as he strode past Philip into the foyer. "I'm your agent, not your bloody babysitter."

"If by plans you mean you intended to haunt Jackson Square and dazzle female tourists with your charming accent, then I imagine the populace of New Orleans would thank me for intervening."

He knew that calling Rupert and essentially demanding that he come over and keep him company tested the boundaries of their professional relationship, but he was supposed to be his friend as well, right?

Furthermore, he'd thought about inviting over a female companion, but after spending dinner with Carrie, he couldn't muster the needed enthusiasm. He tried to tell himself that her unwillingness to adhere to his assistant idea had put him in an ill humor, but he suspected that it had more to do with not wanting to spend the night with a poor substitute.

It'd be like craving Baked Alaska and settling for a snack cake.

Which put him in mind of the dessert she'd mentioned waiting at home. That little tidbit had annoyed him far more than it should have, dammit. What was it to him if she had a guy waiting at home? Nothing…so long as that guy was her brother, or an infirm old uncle, or an impotent friend. But she'd hardly refer to any of the above as dessert, now would she? And that unhappy realization brought him back to his ill humor and sexually frustrated state.

Though he'd managed to cover things well enough—thank God for that nice linen napkin he'd placed in his lap, Philip thought—his loins had been experiencing the fiery blazes of hell all during their meal. Honestly, he'd been amazed at his stark reaction, though in truth now that he thought about it, he didn't know why he'd been so surprised. If he got a hard-on from simply watching her show, then it only stood to reason that being with her was going to have a more potent effect.

And it certainly had.

Though he'd tried his best to be obnoxious and intimidating, he kept getting distracted by the delicate slope of her cheek, the classic arch of her brow and that plump, suckable bottom lip. Every particle of his being had been affected by her presence. His scalp had tingled, his palms had itched, and his belly had suddenly felt as though it had been pumped full of air. It had been most disconcerting.

To make matters worse, he'd felt that odd sense of familiarity with her again and, while it had been curiously enjoyable over dinner, he'd felt the absence of the sentiment the minute they'd parted ways, leaving him at odds and out of sorts.

He'd come home, fixed himself a drink and watched her show. When that had failed to alleviate his gloomy mood, he'd called Rupert. This house was too bloody big, Philip thought, pouring his irritated agent a glass of wine.

"What's this about?" Rupert wanted to know.

Philip shrugged. "I thought you might want to know how things went this evening."

"You could have told me that over the phone," Rupert said. "Why did I have to trot over here? I've got a life, too, you know."

Well, this superb mess was thanks to Rupert's inability to properly ink a contract, so he was just going to have to get over it, Philip thought. "Until this special is over, your life, like mine, is on hold. If I'm going to go to hell in a handbasket, you can bet that I'm not making the trip alone. You're coming along for the ride as well."

Rupert collapsed heavily into a chair. "So that's what this is about. You're lonely again. Why don't you let me call—"

"I'm not lonely," Philip lied churlishly. "And I swear if you suggest calling a hooker for me one more time there's going to be bloodshed."

"They don't call it the Big Easy for nothing," Rupert replied.

"For God's sake, I don't have to pay to get my knob polished," he told him, still annoyed. Him? Lonely? He wasn't lonely, dammit. Lonely implied that he needed someone to make him happy and he didn't. He'd learned to be self-sufficient when his parents had stopped hugging him. He'd learned that there wasn't anything anyone could give him that he couldn't manufacture for himself.

Lonely, hell.

Rupert kicked his feet up on the coffee table. "So, how did it go?" he asked with a somewhat resigned sigh.

"Not well," Philip told him, ready for a subject change.

"I take it she didn't like the idea of being your assistant?"

"No," Philip said with a chuckle, remembering her thin-lipped expression. "It quite pissed her off."

Rupert tutted thoughtfully. "I wish I could say I

was surprised, but honestly, I'm not. These American women are different. Bossy," he said with a puzzled frown. "Did you know there's an entire movement of women from New Orleans who call themselves the Chicks in Charge? It's a club of sorts where bossy women teach other women how to be bossy. I heard a couple of hens clucking about it in line at the grocery yesterday."

A memory stirred, but vanished before he could grasp it. "That sounds familiar," he said, wondering where he'd heard the phrase.

"I don't know what the world is coming to," Rupert lamented. "Women didn't used to be so bloody picky. If it weren't for the whole British thing to set me apart, I daresay I'd be having a hard time finding a woman to occasionally warm my bed." He shot Philip a look. "That's your problem, you know. If you'd just let a pretty bird balance on your balls for a night, I daresay this foul mood of yours would dissipate."

Philip smiled blandly. Getting laid was Rupert's answer to everything. No doubt to some extent he was right, but since the Sophie incident, Philip had been in a sort of hibernating celibacy.

For years he'd enjoyed a healthy sex life, had pretty much dipped his wick as frequently as the urge struck, but something about the Sophie deal—

being made a royal fool of—had put an end to that carefree mentality. He hadn't had a woman since, and to be completely frank, aside from fantasizing about Carrie Robbins, hadn't been interested.

Not to say that he hadn't been horny—men didn't need an excuse to be horny. If the wind blew properly, most men could get it up. But when the urge struck, he merely took matters into his own hands— that whole self-sufficient thing—and there were no complications.

But if tonight's reaction to Carrie was any indication, he could sure as hell anticipate complications for the coming week. Being with her, particularly when he knew she was going to be primped up like a porn star, was undoubtedly going to push him to the brink of sexual insanity.

Philip frowned. "I want you to go back first thing Monday morning before we start and see if you can do anything about her wardrobe." Beating a dead horse, he knew, but he was desperate.

"Philip," Rupert said, heaving a beleaguered sigh. "There's no point. They're not going to budge."

"Just try, would you?" he asked impatiently. He massaged the bridge of his nose.

Rupert studied him thoughtfully. "So that's the way of it then?"

"What are you gabbing about?"

"You're attracted to her."

"Well, of course, I'm attracted to her," Philip snapped. "She's bloody gorgeous and she doesn't wear any clothes. Who wouldn't be attracted to her?"

"I'm not," Rupert said matter-of-factly.

Philip shot him a disbelieving look. "Sod off."

"I'm not," Rupert insisted. "She's too pretty," he explained. "In order for me to be attracted to a woman, I've got to know there's a shot at having her. A girl like that—" he shrugged "—not a chance in hell. She's out of my league, mate."

"But what about fantasies and such?" Philip asked, surprised by his agent's mentality.

"You mean like celebrities? Like if Halle Berry suddenly plucked me off the street and wanted to shag me till my balls turned blue?" He nodded. "Yeah, I have those. But they're fantasies. I know they're never going to happen. See the difference?"

Philip paused. Strangely, he did.

"If you're *attracted* to Carrie, it means you know it could happen, that it's not out of the realm of possibility."

Philip chucked darkly. "Oh, it's definitely out of the realm of possibility."

Rupert arched a brow. "Because she's not interested or because you insist?" he asked annoyingly.

"Both," Philip said, not altogether sure that the

two applied. Frankly, before he'd completely pissed her off, he'd discerned what he thought might be a flicker of interest on her part. He'd deemed it wishful thinking, and hadn't given it another thought.

Until she'd come back to their table and had found Beth in her chair.

Philip smiled. He'd definitely detected a hint of jealousy there, he thought, recalling her tightly controlled outrage.

Now that had certainly been an enlightening exchange. He'd learned a couple of interesting little facts, the first being the aforementioned jealousy. Given the flash of anger in those otherwise calm eyes, Philip knew that his deliberately provoking attention to the other woman had ticked her off.

But what he'd found equally interesting was how swiftly Beth had deemed Carrie a threat. She'd taken one look at her and her expression had gone from polite to icy. She'd disliked her on sight. Carrie had taken it in stride, which told Philip that this was a seemingly regular occurrence. It had to be disheartening to be judged so unfairly, he thought.

To some extent he could see where the *Negligee* costume might actually be an advantage—it gave her anonymity. If she garnered that much attention out of costume, then there would be no end to what she'd get if people truly recognized her.

Regardless, Philip fervently—selfishly—wished that at the very least, they'd dial the sex factor down a notch. Things didn't bode well for his peace of mind, ability to concentrate and his plans to remain self-sufficient otherwise.

She was walking temptation…and he wanted her.

"There's no morals clause this time," Rupert said, as though he'd read his mind.

Bloody hell, Philip thought. There went that excuse.

"ARE YOU SURE ABOUT THIS, Carrie?" Dana—formerly Dan until the marvels of medical science had proven otherwise—asked skeptically. She held the almost completely sheer concoction of pink fabric and feathers by a single spaghetti strap.

Carrie nodded. "I'm sure."

Dana grunted and shot her a bewildered look, then went about steaming the wrinkles out of the piece. She had good reason to be confused. Her wardrobe manager had tried repeatedly to get her to wear the ultra sexy, ultra revealing negligee over the past few months and each time she'd hauled it off the rack, Carrie had shook her head and deemed it too risqué. That she'd come in this morning and specifically asked for the outfit had to throw her for a loop.

"Okay," Dana finally said, apparently unable to quell her curiosity. "What gives? Why now?"

"We're doing a special," Carrie told her. "The theme is *Summer Sizzling*. This outfit says sizzle, right?"

"Don't be coy," her friend said. "I know better. You still flinch every time I spray hairspray on your ass to keep your panties from riding up."

"There's nothing odd about that," Carrie told her. "Why don't I apply hairspray to your ass and see if you don't flinch?"

Dana grinned. "Honey, my ass wouldn't flinch if you applied a cattle prod. Drag Queen U, baby. Where do you think I learned that hairspray trick?" She snorted, handed Carrie the outfit and gestured for her to change behind the curtain. "The last time I tried to get you into this costume you said over your dead body and you look pretty damned *live* to me. Tell the truth. What's happened? What's changed your sweet little anal-retentive modest heart?"

Carrie smiled, struggled into the outfit. After a couple of minor adjustments, she managed to squeeze her breasts into the cups. "My new co-host had some…issues with my wardrobe," Carrie admitted. She stepped out from behind the curtain waited for Dana to lace up the back.

Taking offense, Dana grunted. "What kind of issues?" she demanded.

"Evidently he thought I wasn't wearing enough." She told her about their meeting and his assistant request. How he'd asked to tone down the centerfold image while they were working together.

Dana chuckled, finished knotting the laces so they wouldn't come undone, then slid a finger down Carrie's spine. "Ah, yeah. There it is," she said, as though just making an important discovery.

Carrie frowned, tried to look over her shoulder. "Where what is?" she asked.

"Your backbone. I knew you had one." She nodded approvingly, bent down and tweaked the feathers along the hem of the garment. "Well, baby, this is one case where less is more. You look *hot*. You're going to set the cameras on fire."

Carrie didn't care so much about that as setting Philip on fire—his temper and his libido. The more she'd thought about things over the weekend, the more she'd been convinced that he needed taking down a peg or two. His assistant, she thought again. Good grief. Just where the hell did he get off?

Joyce had also told her that he'd insisted on using her set. That was fine—she was more comfortable there, after all. But why had *his* been off-limits? What made him so almighty that he dictated so much of how this played out? Like he was the only person being inconvenienced? Didn't she have any say?

Obviously he didn't think so, but he'd best think again. And if he hadn't already, he would the minute she walked onto set in *this,* Carrie thought.

"Does this mean that I can pull out all the stops this week?" Dana asked hopefully. "I found a sexy little mocha number in a vintage shop that would make any dog bark, if you know what I mean. I was saving it for myself, but—" she eyed Carrie's cleavage enviously "—you'd definitely fill it out better."

"Bring it in," Carrie told her determinedly. "As long as it covers the essentials, I'll wear it."

Dana shot her a considering look. "Mercy. He must have really pissed you off."

"He did worse," she said grimly. "He underestimated me."

Seemingly impressed, Dana inclined her head. "Get him, baby. Teach his self-important ass a lesson he'll never forget." She coupled a sly glance with a mysterious smile and made a yum noise deep in the back of her throat. "I know there's a few lessons I wouldn't mind teaching him."

"Dana," Carrie admonished.

"What?" she asked. "Like I don't know you think he's hot."

"Dana."

"Don't 'Dana' me," her wardrobe manager said. "You know it's true."

It was, and she couldn't deny it. Still… "That's neither here nor there."

She grunted again. "I'd take him here, there, anywhere. Mercy, that man has one helluva ass. Like a ripe apple," she said with a faraway look. "Now, that's an ass you can sink your teeth into."

Carrie chuckled, slightly outraged. "You're crazy."

"And so are you if you don't take advantage of this opportunity. One look at you in this outfit and he'll be ready to detonate," she said. "Hell, I'm not even a man anymore, but if I still had a penis *you* in *this* would have initiated the launch sequence."

Sweet Lord, Carrie thought as a strangled laugh bubbled up her throat. Her cheeks stung with instant heat. Was there anything she wouldn't say? "I'm flattered…I guess," she said, wondering what the PC response would be to that sort of compliment.

Dana laughed. "Oh, hon. You're such an easy target."

And therein was the problem, Carrie thought. She was tired of being an easy target. Tired of being underestimated, an object of lust but never love, of constantly been leered at and envied, instantly disliked. The incident at Mama Mojo's with Beth sprang unhappily to mind. It shouldn't bother her—she had great friends, the *best*—and yet it did.

She had to stop giving people the power to hurt her, Carrie thought, irritated with herself. She had to stop caring what other people thought and stop apologizing for first being fat, then losing the weight and being pretty.

She'd tried to fix herself on both counts and look what had happened?

After that last miserable year of school—in yet another attempt to blend in or be accepted, she thought bitterly—Carrie had decided that being pretty was overrated. She'd hidden behind her hair, had worn shapeless jeans two sizes too big and shirts that swallowed her. A soft smile tugged her lips.

But then Providence had provided her with the spunkiest, most outspoken roommate she could ever have hoped to have had—Frankie Salvaterra—and the little Italian hothead had bullied her out of her cocoon, had made her realize that as long as she was true to herself, it didn't matter what anyone else thought. In other words, "Screw 'em."

Frankie had no idea of knowing, but Carrie had always felt like she'd saved her that year. She'd started doing things to please herself and had begun to tune out the people who weren't important in her life. Occasionally she'd still revert to old behaviors—like now—but for the most part, she was proud of who she was and who she'd become.

Their next-door roommates had been Zora and April. The four had formed an instant bond—one that she was eternally grateful for because up until then, she'd never had a group of real girlfriends. Their nomadic lifestyle hadn't afforded her the time to form any lasting attachments to anyone and, like she'd said before, high school had been an outright nightmare. Carrie let go a breath.

Bottom line—she was who she was…and she was tired of apologizing for it.

She felt the cool blast of hairspray hit her ass and was proud of herself when she barely twitched. Right now she was *Let's Cook, New Orleans! Negligee Gourmet.*

She'd dressed for the part—the time had come to start playing it.

5

"SO THAT'S THE WAY it'll play out," Jerry was saying. "Just be sure and watch for your minute cues. Time will run out a lot faster with the two of you than you've—"

Jerry stopped short and his gaze was suddenly riveted to something to the left of Philip's right arm. In fact, the entire studio had gone disturbingly quiet.

"—been used to," his producer finally finished in a thinly strangled voice. He cleared his throat.

"Holy mother," he heard one of the camera guys whisper.

"She doesn't look like *my* mother, bro," someone whispered.

Philip knew there was only one reason why the studio would grind to a halt like this—Carrie. Evidently she'd made her entrance and, judging from Jerry's reaction and the other discreet coughs and telling pauses, he knew she must have really pulled out all the stops. Though he equally anticipated and dreaded it, Philip slowly turned 'round.

And immediately wished he hadn't, because he felt a flash-fire engulf his loins and his mouth dropped appallingly open before he'd had the presence of mind to lock his jaw.

"Good morning," she said cheerily as she competently negotiated the various cables strewn along the floor in what had to be five-inch heels.

She wore a tiny pink nightie fashioned out of some alarmingly see-through fabric and feathers. And thank God for the feathers, Philip thought, which strategically covered her breasts. Upon closer inspection, a thicker material lay underneath forming a pair of panties, otherwise she would have undoubtedly had feathers covering her kitty as well. Which called to mind all sorts of cat and canary analogies, Philip thought, doing his best to a swallow a maniacal laugh.

To make matters worse, her hair wasn't snarled up into big waves, but had been left long in sensual curls that cascaded over her shoulders and down her back. In addition, her makeup didn't appear to have been troweled on by an artist channeling Tammy Faye Baker.

Whoever had applied this morning's look knew what they were doing. They'd subtley enhanced her natural beauty by highlighting the most striking features of her face—her eyes and lips. Pale lavender shaded her lids, complementing their violet color, and a soft raspberry glowed on her plump, kissable mouth.

It was a flawless combination of the two, Philip realized—the Carrie he'd met Saturday night and her *Negligee* counterpart. She looked competent, confident, and determined. In fact, he detected not even the slightest hint of nervousness at all.

Curiously, that disturbed him almost as much as the hard-on currently threatening to swell out of his pants.

"Good morning," he finally drawled.

Carrie smiled at him. "I have no complaints so far," she said. "But it's early."

From the corner of his eye he watched Jerry and Joyce share an uncomfortable look. "Well," Joyce said nervously. "Before we get started why don't the two of you inspect the kitchen, familiarize yourselves with each Act."

Carrie nodded, cast him a glance. "Come along," she told him with an imperious little wave which set his teeth on edge. "Since this is my set, how about I show you the layout?"

Philip fell in line behind her. Predictably, his gaze gravitated to her barely covered ass, which somehow only served to irritate him more. "It's still a kitchen," he pointed out. "Last time I checked, I knew my way around one," he drawled sardonically.

"Be that as it may, you don't know your way around *this* one."

Actually, he'd watched her show enough he could undoubtedly navigate it blindfolded but since all that little admission would do was flatter her, Philip decided to keep it to himself.

"Here's the refrigerator, of course," she said, gesturing much like the letter-turner he'd wanted her to be. She ticked off the other major appliances, as well, as though he were too thick to recognize a stove. By the time she'd finished her little demonstration, Philip was seriously considering strangling her with his apron strings.

He glanced at her outfit and hardened even more painfully. "What?" he asked. "Couldn't find any pasties?"

Her lips curled with smug humor. "Those are for tomorrow."

His eyes had bugged before he'd realized she was kidding and she laughed delightedly at his expense. "I'm joking," she said. She crossed her arms over her chest, inadvertently plumping her cleavage. "I think the network would draw a line at pasties."

"Not if it sold advertising," Philip said. "You're playing with fire, you know," he told her.

She merely shrugged, apparently unconcerned. "I play with fire all the time."

Not to this degree, he'd wager. He'd known that he'd pissed her off with his little assistant idea, but he'd honestly not had any idea that he'd angered her into this form of revenge. If he'd had, he'd never have suggested it.

And that's exactly what it was, Philip thought—revenge. He'd asked her to wear more, so to punish him, or put him in his place, or some other crack-brained female notion, she'd decided to torture him by wearing less. His nostrils flared as he pulled in a breath.

And gallingly, it was working.

He'd be lucky if he didn't slice a finger off or set himself on fire. How the hell was he supposed to concentrate when she looked like that? he wondered with furious despair. When all he could think about was popping one of those lush breasts loose of its dangerously unstable cup and making a meal out of her? Of nudging that flimsy fabric clinging to her ass aside and burying himself into her? What a freaking nightmare, he thought. An unholy quagmire of—

"Ready yet?" Jerry called to them.

Philip pushed a hand through his hair. Ready?

No. Resigned? Yes. He summoned a smile. "Certainly."

"What about you, Carrie?" Joyce wanted to know. "Does everything look okay?"

"Looks fine, Joyce. I'm ready when you are."

"Okay," Joyce called. "Places, everyone! Let's make some magic happen."

The studio bustled to life, everyone hurrying to find their respective places. Philip felt Carrie move in beside him and, though it could have simply been his imagination, he suspected that she purposely brushed against him. His dick twitched hard behind his zipper. He closed his eyes tightly shut and swore, tried to think calming thoughts.

"Here we go people," Jerry called. "Three, two, one…"

"Good evening, everyone," Carrie said. "I'm Carrie Robbins, your *Negligee Gourmet.*"

"And I'm Philip Mallory," he smoothly interjected. "Have we got a treat for you. For this week— and this week only—" he decided to emphasize "—Carrie and I are teaming up to bring you special *Summer Sizzling* programming."

Carrie grinned. "If summer's not hot enough for you, then we've got some fantastic meals planned that we guarantee will warm things up around your table…and hopefully other areas of your home as well," she added, her voice loaded with sexy innuendo.

"Guys," Philip confided, "women love a man who knows his way around a kitchen. If your honey isn't feeling the love, treating her to a hot, spicy dish is one surefire way to warm her up."

Carrie smoothly followed the cue. "And ladies, we've all been told the quickest way to a guy's heart is through his belly."

Or more accurately his zipper, Philip thought, with a soft chuckle which caused Carrie to shoot him a look. Who wrote this stuff? he wondered, wishing they could simply ad-lib.

"Today we're going to grill some fresh salmon steaks," Philip said, dutifully following the teleprompter.

"And we're going to enhance that flavor by adding a spicy mango chutney," Carrie added.

"We'll round the meal out with a fresh garden salad and roasted potatoes," he finished.

"If you're interested in seeing what's for dessert, stay tuned," Carrie told their viewers. She shot the camera a distinctly seductive smile. "I promise it'll be worth it."

They cut to commercial and Philip breathed a silent sigh of relief. Jerry hurried up. "That wasn't so bad, was it?" his producer asked hopefully.

That depended on whether or not you asked his dick, Philip thought, which threatened to launch right out of his pants every time she purposely brushed against him.

"The chemistry is fantastic," Jerry went on. "The two of you look amazing together and the dialogue seems natural."

"About that," Carrie said. "Can we ad-lib a little? To me it sounds a bit too rehearsed."

Philip's first impulse was to agree—it was stilted and flowery and frankly, he hated it—but it was better than Carrie ignoring the script altogether. If they gave her carte blanche with the dialogue, who knew what she'd come up with? He shuddered to think.

"Actually, I'd prefer to follow the script," Philip said, shooting her a look that proclaimed his displeasure.

She cocked her head and gave him a wry smile. "Really," she said. "That's odd. Saturday night you weren't interested in following the format at all. Better dialogue makes for a better show. I'm a fairly competent conversationalist. You seem to be as well. What's the problem?"

"There isn't a problem, per se. I just think things would run more smoothly if we followed the teleprompter."

The corner of her ripe mouth tucked into a grin and her eyes sparkled with humor. "More smoothly, eh?"

Philip considered her, then rested a hip against the counter. Instinct told him to let it go, but pride wouldn't allow it. "Yes, more smoothly. You see, I've noticed that you occasionally run off on various unrelated tangents on your show and well…" He offered her an indulgent smile he knew would irritate her. "While it's fascinating that you once met an African shaman who thought rosemary held healing properties, it doesn't exactly apply to the preparation of a meal."

Ah, now that lit her temper, Philip thought, pleased when her cheeks brightened with annoyed color.

"It does when I'm seasoning with rosemary," she said tightly.

He pulled a light shrug. "If you say so."

Rather than argue anymore, Carrie looked to Jerry to settle the argument. His head had been darting back and forth between them as though he'd been following a tennis match.

He flushed, obviously torn. "I don't see any harm in ad-libbing so long as it pertains to the meal," his traitorous producer finally said.

Philip mentally swore and swallowed a resigned sigh. The first battle—a landmark—and she'd claimed it. Unfortunately, he gloomily suspected it was the first of many.

KNOWING THAT IT WOULD infuriate the hell out of him because it was her recipe, Carrie picked up a fork and loaded it for Philip. "You've got to try this," she said as they prepared to round out their show.

Smiling, Philip's eyes widened in warning and he shook his head. "Oh, I'm sure it's wonderful, but—"

Carrie popped the bite into his mouth before he could finish, withdrew the fork and, smiling, waited for him to swallow. She knew he never tried any of his own meals on his show and it bothered her. If food was prepared, it should be eaten. That he wouldn't eat his own stuff was curiously incriminating.

He glared at her. "Wonderful," he said. "An excellent blend of flavors." He glanced at Jerry, noted the fifteen-second cue and smiled. "Thanks for joining us," he said.

"...and be sure and tune in tomorrow," Carrie added. "Another sizzling summer meal that's guaranteed to satisfy one hunger and spark another is on the menu. Until then, best wishes for your *hot* dishes."

"And that's a wrap," Joyce called. She beamed at

both of them and the studio burst into applause. "Fantastic," she enthused. "Loved the ad-libbing, Carrie. It really gave it a personal flair—like the two of you could be friends…or more," she added slyly. A chorus of ooh-la-la's and catcalls erupted on set.

She certainly couldn't deny that. Other than a few little veiled comments, she and Philip had worked together remarkably well.

Of course, that might have something to do with the fact that she'd happily tortured him throughout their session. Plumping her cleavage, accidentally-on-purpose pressing her breasts against his arm, licking her lips. She'd had entirely too much fun watching those silvery eyes darken with arousal, watching him struggle to maintain his composure when it was clear he couldn't decide which he wanted to do more—strangle her or kiss her.

Frankie had *definitely* been right—Philip Mallory, her fantasy guy, wanted her. She smiled and mentally rocked back on her heels.

He didn't want to…but he did.

Jerry watched the final minute on the playback, then hurried over. "Seriously, that was amazing. The perfect blend of camaraderie and tension. This is going to boom, I'm tellin' ya." He slapped Philip on the back and smiled widely at Carrie. "Great job. I'm not kidding. That was *phenomenal*."

Philip shot her a droll look. "I didn't see 'Feed Philip' on the teleprompter."

"Don't worry. You aren't going blind."

"I know that, dammit," he said peevishly. "It wasn't there. I thought you were only going to ad-lib dialogue. Tell me, do you intend to be a renegade host for the rest of the week?"

Carrie chuckled. "R-renegade host?"

He flushed, then scowled. "You know what I mean. I don't like to eat on camera. I don't even sample my own meals."

"I know," she said, crossing her arms over her chest. "It's annoying."

"Annoying?"

"Yes. If you won't even eat it, what's to make a person who's watched your show go to the trouble of cooking it? What's the point?"

"The point is that whether I eat it or not, it's still good."

"But eating it yourself proves that, right?"

His expression blackened further. "Why am I arguing with you?" he asked. "Why in bloody blazes do I care if my eating on camera annoys you or not? Just don't feed me anymore, or I assure you, you won't care for the outcome."

Carrie quirked a brow. "You'll spit it out?"

He smiled wolfishly at her. "Possibly even at you."

An unexpected chuckle bubbled up her throat. "That would call for some serious retribution."

His eyes glinted with wry humor. "I think you're practicing enough of that already, don't you?"

Carrie smiled innocently and looked away. "I have no idea what you're talking about."

He shook his head, laughed and that twinkling gaze caught and held hers. "Oh, but you do. That's why you've shown up here today wearing less than you've ever worn. Why today, I wonder?" he asked with mock bewilderment. "Could it possibly be because I asked you to wear *more?*"

Carrie chewed the inside of her cheek and regarded him with cool amusement. "Have you watched all of my shows?" she asked.

"No," he said, clearing his throat. "Why do you ask?"

"You keep referencing them, that's why."

He shrugged. "Oh, you know how it goes. Keep your friends close…"

"And your enemies closer," Carrie finished, inclining her head as understanding dawned. She swallowed a bitter laugh. So much for hoping he'd actually admired her as a peer. "At what point did I become your enemy?"

"The instant Jerry mentioned the special," Philip told her. "I like things the way they are, Carrie. No matter how well this goes, I don't want to do another show. I want to keep the one I've got."

Since she'd like to have a better one, Carrie didn't bother lying. She merely nodded. "Understood."

Seemingly satisfied, Philip's gaze dropped to her feather-clad breasts, then retraced the path and found her gaze once more. He sidled a little closer to her, purposely invading her personal space. "Furthermore payback's an interesting thing," he said. "It's a door that swings both ways."

Oh, hell, Carrie thought, feeling her heartrate kick into Mach III. She hadn't expected this. Using her own sex appeal as a weapon had been quite liberating, but frankly, if the idea that he might actually turn the tables on her had ever entered her head, she would have left well enough alone.

Carrie swallowed. "It is?"

He sidled even closer. She could feel his heat, could feel every hair on her body arcing toward him as though he had some sort of magnetic appeal. "Definitely," he whispered, those silvery eyes falling to her mouth.

"I'll be sure to keep that in mind," she managed, struggling not to lean into him. That supremely carnal mouth of his was mere inches from hers. If she tiptoed, she could taste him. A fatal mistake, she knew, but God, she'd never been more tempted, or more certain that he'd taste like heaven and hell, sin and salvation. Dark and dangerous, hot and thrilling.

Addictive.

Funny thing about flirting, Carrie realized. With every conceded point she managed to wring from him, her own attraction seemed to inflate and grow. Furthermore, until today, she'd never gotten fully into her *Negligee* role—never truly let her sensual side go the way the network had hoped she would. Oh, she'd done well enough, she supposed. Her ratings were excellent. Fan mail arrived in bulk daily. They had no reason to complain.

But she'd discovered the problem this morning— the reason she'd never fully engaged her *Negligee* persona was because she'd never had a catalyst. Never had any reason to flirt, or preen, or purposely play coy.

Until today.

Until Philip.

Frankly, Carrie had had the time of her life today, watching him struggle to maintain his composure. The naughtier she became, the harder he tried, the more fun she had. It was a fascinating cycle, which had the unwelcome side effect of making her want him all the more.

If he turned the tables on her—started using his own sex appeal as a weapon to combat hers—Carrie knew she'd be in serious trouble. Should he crook his finger, her resistance would sizzle away like water on hot griddle. Evaporate completely. Simply standing next to him did things to her sex that generally didn't happen until well into foreplay.

Take now, for instance. She could feel her heat drenching into the fabric nestled between her legs, a hot steady throb beating at her center. And thank heaven these feathers covered her nipples because they were presently drawn up in tight little nubs, shamelessly puckered for his kiss. An image of that carnal mouth attached to her bare breast materialized in her mind's eye.

Her knees wobbled.

She took the fantasy a step further and imagined using those big hands to set her atop the kitchen island, spreading her thighs and taking her until she couldn't find the strength to breathe, much less stand. Hard and fast, desperate and dirty. In every dream, that's how it had played out.

That's how much she'd wanted him.

Philip smiled, seemingly satisfied that he'd made his point and drew back, thus enabling her to breathe regularly again. He turned and started off set, then paused and shot her a curiously triumphant look. "Hey, Carrie?"

"Yeah," she said shakily, struggling to gather her wits.

"You made one helluva assistant today."

She let her head loll back and laughed. Oh, Lord, what had she gotten herself into? What the hell had she started?

"So did you," she shot back, determined not to let him have the last word.

She only hoped he didn't end up having the last laugh.

6

WELL, NOW, PHILIP THOUGHT as Carrie's tinkling laughter followed him off-set, that had certainly been interesting. He'd suspected that she was attracted to him, but there was nothing like confirmation to make a man feel inordinately better, particularly when his privates had been locked in Satan's own hell for the past hour.

However, seeing those gorgeous violet eyes of hers darken into an even more compelling hue had made every agonizing second of his torture worth it.

Carrie Robbins epitomized beautiful and sexy, but when she was turned on…

Bloody hell, Philip thought as his breath quaked out in a shaky sigh.

Where he'd summoned the wherewithal to pull back—to not kiss her—when every particle of his being had screamed for him to do just that, he'd never know. She'd wanted it, too. He'd watched her lids droop, the pulse-beat in her neck flutter. He'd felt her sweet breath fan against his lips, had tasted it and almost whimpered.

Him. Whimper.

It was insane.

Not to brag, but up until his self-imposed celibacy, Philip had enjoyed countless lovers, had been praised for his skill in the sack. In his opinion, a good lover had to have an excellent sense of timing. He had to be able to recognize the time to kiss, the time to nuzzle, the time to massage, the time to suck, the time to dawdle and the time to make haste.

One false note could ruin the entire melody for a woman, so learning to listen to her—a quick inhalation, a groan of pleasure, a prolonged silence—and being able to appropriately read what each one of those cues meant was an art form that, frankly, he believed British men had honed. Philip grinned. The ability to debauch was practically in their blood, passed down from generations of rakes who'd slaked their lusts upon their wives, mistresses, harlots and courtesans.

Philip himself had lost his virginity at thirteen when a friend's older sister had balled the hell out of him. Naturally, having found the whole experience to his liking, his sexual education hit fast-forward after that. In fact, beyond the first time, he'd pretty much been about getting it as often as he could.

But practice, as they say, makes perfect and he was a relatively bright teen. He'd soon learned that if a girl enjoyed it, she was more interested in having a go with him again and so he'd learned to be patient, to read the signs, and the end result was a skillful lover whose number one priority was satisfying a female. The fact was it didn't take much to make a guy come, but a woman… Ah, a woman had to be coaxed, and getting her there was half the fun.

And getting Carrie there would undoubtedly be a party to end all parties, he knew. Her body looked like it had been created expressly for hot, sweaty sex, for carnal pleasures and erotic fantasies. Philip let go a breath.

And she wanted him.

Was this a new development? he wondered, or like him, had she been secretly wrestling with an attraction? Hell, who knew? And in the end, it really didn't matter. What mattered now was what he planned to do with this new fascinating tidbit of information.

Naturally, his first impulse was to bed her. He was a man, after all, presented with an extraordinarily beautiful woman who clearly wanted him as much as he wanted her. She was bright, funny, a damn good chef, and there was simply something about her that made her far more intriguing than any other female he'd ever come in contact with.

Philip couldn't put his finger on it, but he knew it all the same. He couldn't see the air, but that didn't stop him from breathing, right? Something about Carrie Robbins made his skin tingle, his belly inflate, not to mention that nagging familiarity—for lack of a better explanation—that continually wreaked havoc with his senses. He didn't know her and yet…strangely, he felt like he did.

Every time he saw her he felt like he'd come across a seldom seen but treasured friend. His heart did an odd little flutter that poets had rhapsodized about in lyric and verse for centuries. Those annoyances combined with the unrelenting hard-on were beginning to seriously wear upon his nerves.

At any rate, as much as he'd love to back her up against the wall and take her until his legs wobbled, Philip's memory of what had happened the last time he'd slept with a co-worker was still too stark. Morals clause or not, the idea of being made a fool of once again thawed his dick faster than a popsicle on a flaming grill.

Everything bedamned, that would *not* ever happen to him again.

Since bedding her was out of the question, that

just left option number two. She'd gleefully enjoyed using her considerable sex appeal to drive him stark raving mad today. Since she wanted him, too, why should she have all the fun?

And she'd definitely been having fun, too, Philip thought, recalling the sly little smile she'd sent him when he'd accidentally-on-purpose dropped a whisk so that he could hunker down out of the camera's view and adjust himself. An alarming tent had begun to form on the front of his apron, and he'd just as soon not embarrass himself by showing all of America his penis, thank you very much. Not that he wasn't proud of it, but…

Of course, he wouldn't have to worry about hauling around an enormous hard-on if she'd just wear some damned clothes. Where in the hell had they found that outfit? he wondered furiously. Hookers-R-Us? It was indecent. He seriously didn't know how she'd kept her focus today, but to give her credit, she had.

She'd managed to multi-task their meal, ad-lib the segment and torture him. He grunted, felt a smile tug at the corner of his mouth. Not bad for a day's work, the infuriating she-devil.

Furthermore, though he was *extremely* reluctant to admit it, working with her today had been…quite pleasant. She was warm, funny and knowledgeable.

The time had flown by and, though he knew he didn't have any business thinking about it, he couldn't help but wonder what it would be like to fix a meal with her at home. He could easily cast her in a cozy scene in the kitchen, standing alongside him as they cooked and chatted amiably about their day.

Philip's chest inexplicably tightened and for whatever reason, Rupert's "lonely" comment sprang to mind. A guy would never be lonely with her, he thought, letting go a breath he didn't realize he'd been holding.

Not that he was lonely, dammit, Philip thought, scowling at the direction his thoughts had taken. He merely liked having company every once in a while.

Rupert was waiting for him as he neared his dressing-room door. "Jerry's ecstatic," he said. "Over the moon, thrilled, beside himself and otherwise insane with gratitude that you finally agreed to do the special."

Philip summoned a droll smile and let himself into his dressing room. "I am a team player, after all." He pulled his apron off, hung it on a hook attached to the door and gathered his wallet, keys and cell.

Rupert scowled. "From the looks of things, you may be playing too well."

Philip paused and arched a brow. "What do you mean?"

"Just that he kept going on and on about 'chemistry' and 'heat.'" He shrugged. "I wouldn't want things to go too well if I were you. I'd hate for them to get the idea to *extend* the special. We both know that if ratings are good enough, they could certainly do it. Or pair you up again at a later date," he added.

Tension camped in the back of Philip's neck and he felt his blood pressure boil dangerously close to stroke level. "No, they won't," Phillip told him. "Because per my instruction, you had them add that addendum to my contract which nullifies any future requests for any such special."

Rupert winced. "About that," he said tentatively.

"What about that?" Philip growled.

His face fell. "They didn't go for it."

"What?" Philip exploded.

Rupert flinched, then let go a weary sigh. "They wouldn't budge, Philip. I tried."

"What happened to talking some smack?" he all but wailed.

"I got smacked back."

Thoroughly disgusted, Philip groaned, collapsed heavily into his chair and blew out an annoyed breath. "I need a drink."

"Want me to get one for you?" Rupert asked quickly, evidently seizing upon something that he *could* do, since negotiating a contract in his client's favor didn't seem to be working out.

Philip shook his head. "No. Forget it."

"I just think that you need to dial things back a notch," Rupert suggested. "Do your job…but don't do it quite so well." He hesitated. "I saw her in the hall. So much for asking her to wear more, eh?"

Philip closed his eyes and let his head fall back against the chair. "Clearly that wasn't one of my better plans."

"We all make mistakes," Rupert said soothingly.

Philip snorted.

"She's getting to you, isn't she?"

He lifted his head and glared at him. "You saw her. What do you think?"

Rupert smiled. "I think it's a miracle you don't have a mouthful of feathers."

Philip felt his lips twitch. "Yeah, well, I think it's going to take a bloody miracle to get me through this week."

Rupert wandered to the door, preparing to take his leave and grinned. "I suggest the miracle of sex. It does wonders."

"Sod off," Philip said with a weary chuckle. He needed a miracle, all right—divine intervention to prevent him from sleeping with her.

"THIS ONE AND THIS ONE," Frankie said, pushing forward her favorite two of four petite sandwich samples.

Carrie nodded approvingly and made a note. The cucumber and tropical chicken salad were her picks as well. Frankie currently sat at Carrie's kitchen table, obligingly sampling various items for her wedding reception menu.

After this morning, Carrie had needed something to get her mind off kissing, groping and having wild passionate gorilla sex with Philip.

Or more important, *not* kissing, groping and having wild gorilla sex with Philip.

She'd decided that planning Frankie's reception would fit the bill and had jumped into the kitchen—her safe haven/psych ward—and had attacked the job with an almost desperate furor her friend had undoubtedly picked up on.

But she couldn't help it. When in doubt cook, Carrie thought. She glanced around her retro kitchen and winced. Every surface was covered with delectable treats meant for Frankie. So long as she didn't eat all of this, she should be fine.

At any rate, considering that Frankie's wedding was Saturday, she really didn't need to leave things to the last minute. Aside from the cake, she could pull together enough food to feed fifteen the night before, but she'd never been a leave-things-to-the-last-minute kind of girl.

"This really isn't necessary, you know," Frankie said, eying her speculatively. "I totally trust your judgment."

Carrie poured up three different samples of punch and slid them to her friend. "Be that as it may, this is your special day and I want you to be completely pleased."

Frankie harrumphed, took a sip from the first cup. "So long as Ross shows up, I'm not going to have any complaints."

Carrie shot her friend a droll smile and beat down another burst of envy. "I seriously doubt you have anything to worry about."

Frankie hummed with pleasure as she sampled the second cup. "Me either," she confided. "But we're riding together, anyway." She smiled. "Never hurts to make them feel needed," she said, then gestured to the cup. "I really like this one," she commented appreciatively. "It's different. Smooth."

Carrie made another notation on her pad, then moved on to the various sketches of wedding cakes she'd pulled together this afternoon and handed it to her. "Now for the cake," she said, leaning against her white tiled countertop. "I know a lot of people prefer the butter cream icing, but if it's all right with you,

I think the rolled fondant is classier." Furthermore she had something really special planned for her friend's cake—a sentimental memento—and the fondant would work better for her purposes.

Frankie nodded, idly thumbing through the drawings. Finally, she looked up. "All of these are beautiful. Any one of them would make a fine choice, so I'll leave this completely in your competent hands."

"You don't want to pick one?" Carrie asked, surprised. She fully expected her friend would want to micromanage at least a little. It wasn't in Frankie's character to simply surrender, particularly something as important as this.

Her friend shrugged helplessly. "I've already made the most important choice," she said matter-of-factly. "I chose Ross. We're having a baby. We're going to be a family," she said in a voice that came dangerously close to cracking. "Everything else is secondary."

Well, when you put it that way, Carrie thought, feeling a curious lump of emotion lodge in her throat. Would that someday she would have that sort of perspective. Frankie had gone from Bride-zilla to content mom-to-be with startling rapidity and ease.

"I'm so happy for you," Carrie told her friend. And she meant it from the bottom of her heart.

"That's why I know you'll do a good job. I should

have left it all to the people who really cared about me to start with," she said, wincing with the wisdom of hindsight. She pulled a halfhearted shrug and let go a breath. "As I'm sure you noticed, I got all caught up in having a girly-girly wedding, when what I should have been thinking about and thanking my lucky stars for was the impending marriage. That's what's important and I lost sight of it." She smiled, grimaced. "It's a miracle Ross didn't run screaming for the hills."

Carrie chuckled. "He'd never do that. He loves you."

Frankie smiled, lifted her shoulders in another helpless gesture. "Yeah, he does. Go figure." She pulled in a bracing breath. "And you'll find someone who'll love you, too, you know."

Carrie grimaced, started tidying her kitchen. "Let's just get you married off before we start worrying about me."

"I think we should worry about getting you laid," Frankie told her in her customary frank manner. "Speaking of which, how goes it with sexy Philip? Today was your first day working together, right?"

Carrie nodded. "That's right."

"And?" Frankie prodded demandingly.

And it was fun and amazing and she wanted him more with each passing second. Which irritated the hell out of her when it was clear he thought her show was a crock, that he thought she was some sort of opportunistic bitch out to steal his show. Granted his previous experience no doubt contributed to that fear, but she wasn't that woman. And while she might want a better format, she'd never accept one based on compromising his.

Still, she knew Frankie would appreciate her less-was-more tactic. It had been her idea, after all. She told her friend about Philip's condescending assistant request, then shared his other little comments regarding her attire. She sighed when she finished bringing Frankie up to speed. "In short, he's an arrogant ass."

Frankie chuckled darkly and arched a pointed brow. "Please tell me that you didn't let this go without retribution. Tell me that you took our advice."

Carrie grinned. "I did."

Frankie whooped and slapped her hand on the table. "Oh, thank God. I knew being the world's most infuriatingly calm woman couldn't last forever."

"Hey," Carrie admonished, taking slight offense.

"Sorry, sweetheart. But you know it's true. You've been letting things slide for far too long. Personally, I'm glad that this guy finally pushed you past the breaking point." She smiled, seemingly impressed.

"It's going to be interesting to see what comes out of it."

Interesting wouldn't be her word for it, but she did feel better. Liberated. Energized. It would be curious to see if that energy stayed with her tomorrow, particularly if Philip made good his threat and started combating attraction for attraction.

God help her if he did, Carrie thought. It was hard enough keeping her perspective while she tortured him. If he decided to reciprocate the gesture, she'd undoubtedly turn into a quivering, babbling, incoherent nerve of need. And then there was always the possibility that she'd simply snap and their *Summer Sizzling* programming would have to be X-rated.

Carrie cleared her throat. "I did have fun," she confided, cautiously biting her lip. "Being a pain in the ass was quite entertaining. Who'd have thought?"

Frankie grinned. "I've always enjoyed it," she said with a modest bat of her lashes. "I'll have to watch your show. This sounds like it's too good to miss."

"Yeah, well, be sure and tune in tomorrow," she told her. "I have a feeling that's when things are going to really get interesting."

Her friend's eyes sparkled with a do-tell kind of humor. "Oh?" she asked. "And pray tell why is that?"

"He's realized that I'm, er, *slightly* attracted to him and—"

"Only slightly, eh?"

Carrie blushed. "—and informed me this afternoon that two could play my game."

Frankie chuckled delightedly. "Oooh, I wonder if he'll come to work in a Speedo?" she asked, relishing this new turn of events.

She certainly hoped not, Carrie thought, remembering the impressive tent at the front of his apron. Her mouth inexplicably parched and a shiver of heat tingled in her sex. Quite frankly, she didn't think there was enough material in a Speedo to hold him. That erection—and knowing that she'd caused it— had plagued her all damned day. It was bad enough being obsessed with his ass, but imagining full frontal nudity absolutely made every cylinder of her libido fire like it was juiced with liquid nitrogen.

In all honesty, Carrie knew this attraction—this need, pull, drive—to land him between her thighs was unlike anything she'd ever experienced. She'd never questioned her ability to maintain control—to think before she acted. With Philip, she instinctively knew that wouldn't happen. If he lit her up, she'd lose control and they'd both undoubtedly end up roasted as a result of the inferno. Gave a whole new meaning to "Feel the burn," she thought, her lips quirking with dreaded humor.

The thing was, if she thought for one minute that she could simply sleep with him and move on—that she could somehow inoculate herself from the attraction with one round of hot, back-clawing sex, she'd do it in a heartbeat. No question. She'd be on him like white on rice.

But for whatever reason—self-preservation, most likely—she knew that wasn't the case. There'd been something that had drawn her to him from the very beginning. Before she'd ever even met him. She'd felt this curious pull, an odd connection that she'd often spun elaborate fantasies around.

Despite their differences, working with him today had only compounded that feeling. And as much as she was attracted to him, she enjoyed working with him—simply being around him—even more.

Considering that they'd spent a grand total of five hours together over the past few days, that told her that she was in way over her head. He was way out of her league. And she was in imminent danger of losing her heart.

Simply put…she liked him too much.

Her gaze slid to Frankie, to the serene glow of knowing she was loved on her friend's face. That's what she wanted, Carrie thought, swallowing a wistful sigh. What she knew she'd end up wanting from him. Crazy? Premature? Ridiculous?

Yes, all of the above.

But it didn't matter. She knew her own mind—twisted as it was—and she knew beyond a shadow of a doubt that she couldn't just sleep with Philip Mallory and be done with it.

She'd want the total package.

And, if she had to guess, despite the fact she could tell he was reluctantly enjoying himself in her company, depressingly, she'd say he was only interested in untying her bow.

7

"LOTS OF PEOPLE LIKE TO BUY nuts which have already been shelled," Carrie was explaining, much to Philip's humorous chagrin, "but if I have the time, I prefer to shell them myself." She gave a hard squeeze, then a gratifying smile curled her lips as the shell ultimately cracked. She shot Philip a little triumphant grin which competently telegraphed the double entendre she intended.

No doubt it was his balls she'd love to put in a vise and crack, he thought, silently enjoying himself.

He chuckled. "Maybe we should forget calling you *The Negligee Gourmet* and retitle your show *The Nutcracker,*" he teased, knowing it would irritate her.

She merely smiled. "Are we using a flambé technique to grill our spicy pork tenderloin?"

"Er…no," Philip replied, not sure where she was going with this. She'd taken the ad-lib thing to a whole new level this morning, had basically avoided the teleprompter altogether.

She blithely sprinkled the nuts over her salad. "Then maybe you should stop worrying about how I crack my nuts and put out your fire."

She said it matter-of-factly, as though him setting things on fire in the kitchen were a regular occurrence, which is why it took several seconds for his brain to process what she'd implied. His gaze belatedly darted to the grill, where five-inch flames licked up the sides of their tenderloin, slightly charring the outside.

Philip mentally swore, then quickly—smoothly, lest their viewers suspect he didn't know what he was doing—grabbed the mister they kept on hand for these very instances and gave the grill a couple of squirts. Steam billowed as the flames died down.

Good Lord, Philip thought, shaken that he'd made such a rookie mistake.

"Ah, now that ought to do the trick," he said in his most professional voice. "We want to get those flavors *locked in*," he explained. "An excellent sear is always welcome."

"And if you aren't sure how to get an excellent sear," Carrie chimed in as she worked on her vinaigrette, "just burn it a smidge," she instructed. "A little char makes things more interesting, wouldn't you say?" she asked Philip.

It wasn't charred, dammit. It was just a little… crispy. He shot her a tense smile, turned the meat to a more flattering angle for the camera. "Always," he said for lack of anything better.

Carrie finished up her vinaigrette, plated her salad, summer vegetable medley and hot roll. Meanwhile, Philip removed the tenderloin from the grill and started carving it into medallions. An unwelcome crunch sounded every time he sawed through the meat, a condemning noise which told everyone in the studio and at home that he had indeed burned it.

A stinging litany of obscenities streamed though his head. Mortification stung his cheeks, and to make matters worse, Carrie—damn her barely covered ass—had sidled up next to him, purposely angling her breast against his arm. It was no freaking wonder he'd burned the damned thing, Philip thought, his mind an embarrassed quagmire of irritation. What man could possibly work, much less cook, under these conditions?

After yesterday's feather fiasco Philip hadn't thought that she could wear anything that would distract him any more.

He'd thought wrong.

Today's ensemble was decidedly worse. She wore a black and red bustier-type outfit which vaguely reminded him of the old Wonder Woman garb. It was tight, formfitting and satiny.

But that's where the similarities ended.

Carrie's laced up the front and tiny little cut-outs lined the tops of the cups, giving a daring peek at her creamy flesh. He imagined dipping his tongue into each opening, then springing the tie nestled at the heart of her cleavage and allowing those gorgeous orbs to pop free, thereby granting him ultimate access.

"Oh, that smells good," Carrie said, thankfully derailing that erection-exploding line of thinking. Beads of sweat had begun to pop out on his forehead. Christ, he was beginning to lose it.

"Why don't you slip a couple of pieces of that onto the plate?" she told him.

Philip's eyes refocused and he realized that he'd continued to carve the tenderloin when in fact he only needed two slices to add to their demo plate.

He'd screwed up. Again.

Forcing his lips into a snarling smile, he dutifully added the meat to the plate. "Ah, now," he said, once again trying to sound like he knew what he was doing. "That's a fine meal."

"Hopefully a prelude to better things," Carrie said

with a suggestive wink, effectively wrapping up their show. "Until tomorrow, best wishes for *your* hot dishes."

Joyce called the session a wrap and Philip slouched against the counter, massaged the bridge of his nose and swore.

Still provokingly too close, Carrie tutted softly under her breath. "Such language."

Philip glanced up and caught her slightly mocking smile. "You're really enjoying yourself, aren't you?"

She preened. "Yes, actually, I am."

"Not to worry about the small fire, Philip," Jerry said briskly as he hurried over. "The tenderloin still looked wonderful."

"It wasn't *on fire,*" Philip said tightly. He scowled. "There were just a few high flames."

Jerry smiled. "Right. Well. Excellent show. We're already fielding tons of e-mail and a couple of the local shock jocks are talking up the show."

Rupert's dial-it-down-a-notch warning echoed in the wake of Jerry's enthusiasm, causing Philip's abominable mood to blacken even further.

Joyce wandered over to applaud their performance as well. She beamed at them. "Wonderful show, guys. Carrie, you're so relaxed and you look like you're having a ball." She smiled, seemingly marveling at the change. "And you're much more at ease in your *Negligee* costume. Who would have thought putting a guy on set with you would loosen you up? Frankly, my concern was that you would be more uncomfortable—" her gaze slid to Philip "—but clearly I was wrong." She paused, then aimed a you-sly-dog smile at Philip. "Philip, as always, you're fantastic. I liked the distracted-by-my-sexy-co-host bloopers, by the way. Splendid touch." She went over tomorrow's game plan, then finally took her leave. The rest of the studio emptied out, leaving them alone once again.

So much for coming in this morning and giving her tit for tat. Actually, he'd managed to zing her a little before he'd become too befuddled. He'd purposely slid in behind her, bumping her rear with his hip as he walked past her and had enjoyed listening to her breath catch. Unfortunately, when he'd come up with the brilliant plan of pitting her sex appeal versus his, Philip hadn't factored in what he belatedly realized would be the fly in the ointment.

Flirting with her—watching her response to his carefully veiled ministrations—only heightened his own arousal.

In short, he'd stupidly increased his own suffering.

Though he wouldn't have thought it was possible,

he wanted her even more now than he had before he'd initiated his own form of payback. Irritation and pure sexual need tangled his insides into a knot of futile despair. How the hell was he supposed to resist her? How was he supposed to concentrate when every cell in his body screamed for release? Begged him to end his suffering and slake his endless lust against her soft, welcoming body?

Philip glared moodily at her—at that plump carnal mouth, specifically—and felt a bead of moisture leak out of his dick. Though he knew he was too vain, he grimly entertained the idea of tearing his hair out.

This was *her* fault, he decided.

It was her fault he wanted her.

Her fault that he'd been roped into this special.

Her fault that he'd burned the tenderloin.

His gaze slid over her mouth once more and a wave of stark need bombarded him, weakening his knees. His stomach fluttered and another bomb of heat detonated in his loins.

She needed to be punished, Philip thought, sidling in closer to her.

Carrie's gaze shot to his own mouth, then bumped up and tangled with his. "Philip?" she asked questioningly.

"You only have yourself to blame," he said, as

though everything up to and beyond this point were a foregone conclusion. "You win."

"Win what?"

"Me," he said. He backed her against the counter, enjoyed the commingled flash of trepidation and want light up her gorgeous almost-purple gaze.

"B-but I don't want you," she sputtered, as though finally realizing what he was about.

Philip chuckled confidently under his breath, and for the first time since this all began, he finally felt himself slip back into control, knew how to wrestle back the upper hand. Granted he'd made many mistakes with her, but this was one area he knew his own expertise.

And he knew beyond a shadow of a doubt that she wanted him.

"Liar," he said. "Here. I'll prove it."

Then before she could utter another protest, he cupped her face with his hands and swiftly lowered his mouth to hers.

EXACTLY THIRTY SECONDS before Philip's lips connected with hers, Carrie had realized that she'd finally pushed him too far.

She'd watched his face morph from anger to epiphany, then from calculating to determinedly resigned and confident. He'd invaded her personal space, nudged her up against the counter and those liquid silver eyes had darkened with sleepy sexual purpose. If she'd ever seen anything so wonderfully thrilling, she couldn't recall it.

"You win," he'd said and though a small part of her was terrified at what exactly she'd won, another part was secretly thrilled and did a triumphant little happy dance deep within her soul.

Then he'd kissed her and her soul had shattered.

The meeting of their mouths exceeded every expectation, surpassed every dream, obliterated every fantasy.

There was nothing sweet or reverent about the way he kissed her. It was a no-holds-barred full-fledged confident invasion that sucked the air from her lungs, removed every thought from her head and made her heart feel like it was going to pound right out of her chest. Those big hands of his—the very ones she'd found so damned sexy—were currently caressing her face, pushing into her hair.

Her entire body vibrated with relief, sang with tension, tingled with impossible recognition.

She'd never kissed him before, and yet the very taste of him was so welcome and comfortable that she mewled with pleasure.

Philip groaned into her mouth, a heady sound that made her inordinately thankful that the counter was at her back. She greedily ate it up, savored the warm intoxicating taste of him. The hair at the nape of his neck was smooth tangled between her fingers and she could feel a mouthwatering bulge nudge impatiently against her belly.

Her nipples pearled against the slinky fabric of her bustier, sending little tendrils of fire curling through her all the way down to her weeping sex. Her womb clenched, coating her folds with hot joy juice. Her clit throbbed with each expert touch and her skin suddenly felt too tight for her body.

His tongue slid against hers, back and forth, a desperate mimicry of what she longed for between her legs. Seemingly sensing her thoughts and blessedly out of his mind—they were in the set kitchen, for pity's sake—Philip lifted her up and set her on the counter. He settled himself between her legs, the pressure exquisitely perfect against her burning sex.

She looped her arms more tightly around his neck, clung to him and shamelessly shifted forward in a desperate attempt to align him more firmly against her body. If she could have burrowed beneath his skin, she would have. That's how much she wanted him. How much she needed him.

He anchored those wonderful hands on her hips and held her firmly against him, then rocked slightly back and forth, causing a bright sparkler of sensation to ignite deep in her womb. Carrie felt her thighs go rigid, her spine boneless and she melted even closer to him.

Philip's talented mouth cut a path to her ear. "God, you taste so good, Carrie."

She moaned her approval, unable to summon the wherewithal to speak.

He trailed kisses down her neck, sucked and licked, tasted and savored until he reached the delicate cut-outs around the tops of her breasts. Then those eyes darkened again and a hint of a smile curled his lips. He lowered his head and slipped his tongue into each opening, lightly tasting her through the satiny fabric. Carrie gasped, kneaded the muscles in his shoulders, silently telegraphing her approval.

"Ahem."

Somewhere in the dimmest recesses of her mind a warning bell sounded, but she was too caught up in the tornadic cocoon of sexual sensation to heed it. Philip was currently loosening the tie between her breasts with his teeth and his hot breath against her skin prevented her from focusing on anything other than the pleasure she knew was to come.

"A-*hem*."

The tie gave way, causing her breasts to almost tumble from the tiny shelf of fabric concealing them.

Philip's teeth had just latched onto the material when an impatient British voice penetrated their sensual haze.

"Oh, for pity's sake. Must I get the hose?"

Philip went completely still, then closed his eyes tightly shut and swore. Carrie's gaze darted over his shoulder and connected with that of an amused man she vaguely recognized. The accent belatedly registered and she made the connection.

Philip's agent.

"I'll meet you in my dressing room, Rupert," Philip said without turning around, his voice strangled with irritation. That they'd been interrupted, Carrie wondered, or that he'd kissed her to start with?

Her cheeks caught fire. Mortified, she slowly removed her hands from his shoulders and attempted to repair the laces at the front of her bustier.

"I've been waiting patiently for you in your dressing room, but when you didn't show up I thought I'd better come and see if anything was amiss." He smiled and his eyes twinkled with mirth. "Clearly it's not."

"Rupert," Philip snapped. *"Go away."*

"Oh, fine," his agent replied unrepentantly. "It was nice to see you, Ms. Robbins," he said, shooting her another glance that made her wonder just how much of her he'd actually seen. She imagined that Philip's head had blocked most of her from view, but who knew how long he'd been standing there? They'd certainly done quite a bit of moving around—hell, she'd been slithering all over him. God knows what—

In a considerately tender gesture, Philip drew back and helped her right her clothes. All she'd managed to do was tie the damned thing in a knot.

"Sorry about that," he said, his voice somewhat rusty. His molten gaze tangled with hers. "I forgot that Rupert would be by this afternoon. Are you okay?"

"Embarrassed," Carrie admitted, still wishing for a convenient hole to open up beneath her. "But otherwise unharmed."

Philip nodded. "Good." He paused, somewhat nervously. "What are you doing this evening?" he wanted to know. "I, uh… I think we should get together and talk."

That could be interpreted several different ways, Carrie thought, wondering which one he intended. "I'll be at home tonight. I'm catering a small wedding for a friend this weekend and I've got to get some of the prep work done."

"Would I be in the way if I came over?"

"No," Carrie replied cautiously, feeling a curious swooping sensation wing through her abdomen.

"Sixish, then?"

She licked her swollen lips. "That sounds fine."

Philip smiled, effectively snatching what was left of her breath from her lungs, then helped her down from the counter and pressed another lingering kiss to her still tingling mouth. "See you tonight," he said, before turning to walk away.

Miraculously, a thought struck when it didn't seem possible that she'd even have two to rub together. "Wait! I, uh… I need to give you my address."

Philip shot her a look over his shoulder and a sexy chuckle rumbled up his throat. "I know where you live."

She frowned, surprised. "But—"

"Keep your friends close…" he said significantly.

And your enemies closer, Carrie silently finished. The question was, which one was she now?

Better still, which one would she be tonight?

8

PHILIP BARGED THROUGH his dressing-room door and speared Rupert with a glance. "What the hell were you thinking?"

"I was thinking with my brain." His agent grinned and plucked a nonexistent piece of fuzz from his coat. "You, evidently, were thinking with another appendage."

"You should have left," Philip snapped, uncharacteristically annoyed over what his agent had just seen. He shoved his hands through his hair. "You embarrassed the hell out of her."

"Really?" Rupert asked. "Considering those outfits she wears, I wouldn't have thought that was possible."

One had absolutely nothing to do with the other, Philip thought, irritated all the more. What a sexist damned thing to say. He told Rupert as much, garnering his agent's speculative attention.

"You're overwrought," he said, eyeing him closely.

"Is it because I interrupted what was obviously the prologue to a sporting sexual encounter and no man enjoys that sort of interruption?" His gaze sharpened. "Or is her lady's honor the culprit behind your ill humor?"

"It doesn't make any difference," Philip told him, not interested in pursuing the latter idea, which he grimly suspected was the predominant sentiment of the two. "What was so bloody important that you had to hang around, anyway?"

Rupert stood. "Nothing, in particular. I have plans tonight and didn't want you calling, demanding that I come over so that you can rant and rail about how abysmal this special is. I'm going to chill with my honey, and like you, I don't appreciate being interrupted."

"Yes, well, I have plans tonight as well, so chill away." Though frankly he should call him just for the hell of it, the moron. Good grief. He'd been seconds away—a mere nod of his head—from sampling those delectable breasts which had plagued every sleeping and waking dream for the past year. Almost and yet—

"Who do you have plans with?" Rupert asked slyly. "A date with the Nutcracker, perchance?"

Yanked from his thoughts, Philip scowled. What?

he wondered. Had Rupert hung back in the shadows and watched the show?

"I got here early and caught a whiff of the fire," his agent explained, seemingly reading his thoughts. "I thought I'd better come and have a look."

Philip's face flushed. "It wasn't a fire, dammit."

"They disabled the smoke alarms. Otherwise the whole set would have been ringing."

"Bloody hell."

"I told you to bed her and be done with it. You're not going to be able to think straight until you do."

Though it was a somewhat cold suggestion, Philip knew the truth lay in it. Quite honestly, he didn't know what had happened a few minutes ago. One instant he'd been seething mad and the next he'd had a mouthful of Carrie, supposedly in punishment for her making him crazy. What sort of bent logic had led him to that plan of action? he wondered, beginning to seriously question his lucidity.

The problem was, he didn't think either one of them were feeling chastened. And speaking strictly for himself, he knew that for those few minutes while he'd made a meal of that succulently sweet mouth and soft, curvy body, he hadn't been feeling much of anything aside from a curiously bizarre sense of recognition—the same one which had plagued him before—and intense urge to plant himself between her thighs, consequences be damned.

In fact, though he didn't appreciate Rupert's insensitive interruption, a small part of him was eternally grateful that he had, otherwise he would have most likely taken her right there.

Had anyone else walked in on them, he imagined they both would have been a damned sight more embarrassed than what they currently were. Rupert, at least, would keep his mouth shut, which would help keep rumors to a minimum.

Not that they hadn't already started, Philip thought with a disgusted snort. He'd heard a couple of little comments this morning when he'd come in—one from a sous chef in the kitchen, another from a camera guy. Already the buzz of their "chemistry" was making the rounds.

Given the fact that he'd like to keep things as low key as possible to prevent possibly losing his show or doing another special, the gossip certainly wasn't helping his cause. Honestly, the less said about all of it the better. Philip released a pent-up breath.

Which was why when he went to Carrie's tonight he would apologize for his lapse in judgment and promise henceforth to keep things on a strictly professional level.

Every cell in his body rebelled at this thought—

particularly the very hard ones currently straining against his zipper—but, logically, he knew it was for the best. Morals clause or not, he simply didn't need to let things progress any further. If he were to do what he really wanted—i.e., take her six ways till Sunday, until every last vestige of lust had been wrung from both of their limp bodies—he knew there would be emotional consequences he'd heretofore never had to deal with.

The kiss to end all kisses had told him that.

Philip had never been in love. He'd liked women before, certainly been in relationships where he quite fancied a girl, but as far as ever feeling the powerless, all-consuming do-or-die sentiment, he'd never felt it. Never experienced anything more than a bit of mild regret over a failed relationship, the inconvenience of having to exert the effort to find a new lover. Shallow? Probably. But that was an honest assessment.

Carrie, he instinctively knew, would be different.

The instant he'd touched his lips to hers he'd felt a curious melting sensation around his heart. His skin had prickled, his scalp had tingled and a bone-deep shiver of recognition had quaked him to the core. He'd felt that same sort of coming-home feeling in her arms as he did every time he walked through the doors of his island villa. Contentment. Peace. Affection.

Factor in that he'd wanted to devour her and he knew he was in trouble.

Quite frankly, Philip would cite the fear of another Sophie debacle to Rupert—possibly even try to convince himself of it—but he knew that it was a convenient excuse. The truth was Carrie Robbins—the level of emotion she'd managed to evoke in such little time—scared the living hell out him. He was so used to being in control, of managing the people around him that the idea of giving anybody the power to possibly hurt him made his gut involuntarily clench with dread.

He was suddenly eight again with a scraped knee, waiting for the taken-for-granted kiss from his mother that never came. Ten when his dog died and there wasn't a shoulder to cry on, only a harsh comment from his father to "stop blubbering over a worthless pup." It was only a dog, he'd said, as if that had somehow lessened Philip's attachment to it. That dog had been his only source of affection for years and he'd loved it to distraction. He'd never had another one. Too painful to subject himself to the eventual guaranteed loss.

He shook his head in a vain attempt to clear the memories from his mind, wishing that he could permanently erase them. He hated this feeling. Helpless. Wounded. This was precisely why he avoided things like this.

And so what if he was occasionally lonely? Philip thought. Lonely was preferable to heartbroken, right?

Right, dammit.

He couldn't let her do this to him, Philip thought. Yes she was beautiful—more lovely than any person he'd ever seen—and yes he wanted her more desperately than he'd ever wanted another woman. And yes the idea of spending any time with her made his blood pressure spike with anticipation and joy. For all of his protests over this special, he couldn't wait to get to work this morning. Couldn't wait to step on set because he knew she'd be there.

Friends close and enemies closer, he thought. What the hell did a guy do when a woman ended up being both?

CARRIE HAD SPENT the better part of the afternoon trying—very unsuccessfully—to not think about what had happened between her and Philip this morning.

Naturally, that endeavor had been an utter failure.

She still couldn't believe how swiftly things had progressed from a hot-lipped kiss to her bustier being undone and Philip's wonderfully talented mouth mere centimeters from her still disappointed nipple. Had his agent—who'd looked entirely too delighted at their indiscretion for her comfort—not walked in when he had, who knows what might have happened?

Who knows? hell, Carrie thought. She knew.

She knew that if they hadn't been interrupted Philip would have made quick work of her bustier and quicker work of the handy, easy-access snaps between her legs…and she would have enjoyed the first orgasm she'd had in almost a year.

Carrie resisted the renewed urge to whimper.

The barely functioning logical part of her brain appreciated the interference. After all, having sex with a co-worker on set clearly wasn't a professional thing to do.

But the illogical part of her thinking—unfortunately the part in control—had wanted to wail and scream and cry. Wanted to pitch an outright temper fit like a sleepy toddler who'd missed her nap.

There were a dozen reasons why sleeping with Philip Mallory should be out of the question, but for the life of her, ever since he kissed her this morning, she hadn't been able to come up with even one.

And he'd be here, at her house, any minute now.

Carrie swallowed a quick gulp of wine and shook her hands out, trying unsuccessfully to shake off the tremors. From his bed in the corner of the living room, Hoover lifted his fluffy white head. Probably wondering if she'd lost her mind, Carrie thought. "Oh, go back to sleep, you little lump of fur," she said, bending down and giving the dog an affectionate pat.

Okay. She could do this, Carrie thought, trying her best to channel her CHiC courage. Frankie, Zora and April wouldn't be nervous, she told herself. Were any one of them in her position, they'd embrace the spirit of their girl-power movement and do as Frankie suggested—cook with something besides gas.

As it was, she'd just been cooking.

Carrie's lips quirked. What could she say? It soothed her. Lots of women tended to bake when they were nervous or overwrought. Or sexually frustrated and miserable.

A knock sounded at her door, inadvertently punctuating the thought. Hoover bolted from his bed and started barking wildly, spinning in circles, then jumping up on her legs. "Calm down," she admonished. "He's not an intruder. He's a friend."

Carrie took a deep bracing breath, smoothed her hands over her thighs and quickly made her way from the living room to the front door. Predictably, Hoover continued his yelping waltz all the way there.

"Hi," she said, standing back so that Philip could walk past. She caught a decadent whiff of his aftershave as he moved inside—something musky and masculine—and she resisted the urge to bite her fist.

Philip smiled rather sheepishly and the idea that he too was a tad nervous made her feel slightly better. "Hi, yourself," he said, bending to offer his hand to her growling dog. He scored points for that, Carrie thought. She didn't trust a guy who didn't like animals. "Who's this?" he asked, gesturing toward her little bichon frise.

"Hoover. He's a bad-ass until you pet him, then he's putty in your hands."

He scratched the dog behind his ears, looked up and smiled. "Hoover, eh? As in J. Edgar?"

Carrie crossed her arms over her chest. "No. As in *vacuum cleaner*. He eats anything that makes its way onto the floor."

Philip chuckled, gave her thrilled dog another fond pat, then slowly straightened. "I had a dog once—a mastiff. He was… He was hit by a car when I was ten. It was dreadful."

"Oh, I'm sorry," she said, instinctively wincing for his pain. "You've never had another?"

Philip sighed and a sad smile shaped his lips. "'There is sorrow enough in the natural way from men and women to fill our day, but when we are certain of sorrow in store, why do we always arrange for more? Brothers and Sisters, I bid you beware of giving your heart to a dog to tear.' "

"Kipling, right?" Carrie asked, touched that he'd memorized such a beautiful poem.

Philip nodded. "The Power of the Dog." He gazed almost wistfully at her puppy. "Hard when we lose them, eh?" He flushed, evidently thinking that he'd said too much. "You're sure you're not too busy?" he asked, casting an idle look around her foyer.

"Not at all," she said, a little unnerved. She called the dog, then started toward the kitchen, gesturing for him to follow her. No doubt they'd both be more comfortable, she thought, then realized that technically wasn't true—her bedroom offered the ultimate luxury. She couldn't imagine anything more comfortable than a soft bed at her back and Philip's hard body hovered above her. Unless, of course, she considered his hard body *beneath* her and then… Carrie resisted the urge to fan herself.

"Wow," Philip said as they passed through the dining room and entered her kitchen. He glanced up and whistled at the ornate copper ceiling tiles. "Now those are gorgeous."

Hoover trundled over, nudged his food around the bowl and when Honey Nut Cheerios didn't magically appear, he lost interest and found his bed. He had one in almost every room.

Carrie's lips curled in an indulgent smile at the dog, then she glanced at Philip. "Thanks. The tiles are original. The previous owner—a friend of mine's husband—had the entire place completely restored."

He nodded appreciatively. "He did an excellent job."

Carrie chuckled and shook her head. "Trust me, Ben Hayes wouldn't settle for anything less."

Philip shot her a startled look. "Ben Hayes, the photographer?"

Carrie wasn't surprised that he'd heard of him. Ben was a local celebrity of sorts. "One and the same." She sighed.

"He does beautiful work," Philip said, settling himself at her kitchen table. "I've got a print of his— the one of the tree. Quite compelling. I'm sure you've seen it."

Carrie offered him a glass of wine and slid a cheese and fruit tray toward him. "Oh, yeah," she said with another quiet laugh. She gestured to the slight mess around her kitchen. "Another friend is getting married beneath that tree this weekend."

His eyes widened. "That's the wedding you're catering?"

"It is."

He snagged the notepad she'd sketched Frankie's cake on and looked it over. "That's gorgeous," he said. "Fondant right?"

Carrie nodded, propped her hand beneath her chin. "Yeah. I like the smooth texture."

"It's a challenge to work with."

Her lips twitched. "I'm quite capable," she said, somewhat defensively.

Philip shot her a look and laughed, the sound rich and intimate between the two of them. "Of that I've no doubt." He glanced at the drawing again. "The hummingbird is a nice touch, better than a bloody dove. I don't think I've ever seen it done before. Marzipan or sugar?"

"What do you think?" she quipped.

"Sugar, definitely. It's the most difficult of the two."

She selected a strawberry. "Am I that predictable?"

"No," he said, thoughtfully considering her. "You're just that stubborn. I've watched you work. You never do anything in half measures."

"What would be the point?"

"Efficiency?" he offered.

"I'm efficient, too."

"And very modest, I've noticed," he teased, those silvery eyes sparkling with humor.

Carrie laughed, easily relaxing as a result of their playful banter. Philip looked quite at home in her kitchen. He wore a pale green linen shirt which complemented his unique coloring and a pair of loose khaki shorts. It was the first time she'd ever seen him out of his proper work clothes and the end result was a guy who looked classy yet comfortable, both in his clothes and in his skin.

His hair was slightly mussed, as though he'd run his fingers through the messy waves, and that wonderfully wicked mouth of his was presently curled in a slight smile. He caught her staring and she had the privilege of watching those pewter eyes darken and droop.

"Er…so why a hummingbird?" he asked abruptly. "I assume it has some special significance for the fair bride?"

Carrie blinked and cleared her throat. "It does. Ross, her fiancé, gave her a stained glass hummingbird when they were dating. He said it reminded him of her—strong but delicate. The perfect combination of beauty and strength." Carrie slid a finger over her drawing. "He was right."

Philip nodded thoughtfully. "Sounds like your friend has met the right guy."

"I think so," Carrie told him. Her lips slid into a self-deprecating smile. "Out of the four of us, I'm the only one left unattached. The only CHiC without a rooster."

"A rooster?" he scoffed as though insulted. "For future reference, I'm certain that any man who wants to attach himself permanently to you will take exception to being compared to the least intelligent of the barnyard animals. Call him a *stallion,* for pity's sake," Philip said with a manly beat of his chest. He shook his head. "A rooster. Preposterous."

A deep laugh bubbled up Carrie's throat and she felt her eyes mist with mirth. "You missed the CHiC reference," she explained. "My friends and I are the founding members of Chicks in Charge. You might have heard of it."

Philip's eyes bugged and a strangled laugh burst from his throat. "Ch-chicks in Charge?" he sputtered. "The bossy women's movement?"

Carrie feigned offense. "Not bossy," she explained patiently. "*In charge.* There's a difference."

Philip tossed his head back and laughed until his sides heaved. "Oh, this is rich. Wait un-until I tell R-Rupert."

His agent? Carrie wondered. What interest in Chicks in Charge could his agent possibly have? She chewed the corner of her mouth and shot him a questioning glance.

Philip caught her look and tried to flatten his smile. "He was telling me about it," he explained. "Wait until he hears that you're one of them. And not just one of them—a founding member." Evidently unable to control himself, he chuckled again. "Sorry," he said. He coughed. "Really. I'll stop now." He darted a speculative look in her direction. "That explains a lot. On the surface you seem quite manageable, but that's hardly the case. You're a crafty CHiC," he said, with a reluctantly impressed smile. "And actually, that would have been a handy little piece of information to have *before* we met for dinner last Saturday night. I would have used a different tack."

Carrie laughed and cocked her head. "You mean you wouldn't have tried to make me be your assistant?"

"Definitely not," Philip said promptly. "I would have coaxed you into thinking it was your idea."

She harrumphed under her breath. "Do you really think that would have worked?"

Philip winced. "Probably not."

Carrie took another sip of wine, felt the heady warmth of the alcohol loosen her limbs. And her tongue. "Is working with me all that bad?" she teased softly.

Philip's gaze caressed her face, skimmed over her mouth. "No," he reluctantly admitted. "Surprisingly not." He let go a breath. "You're excellent at what you do. You'll never hear me say otherwise." His brow furrowed. "It's just…"

"The clothes," she finished knowingly and, for whatever reason, found herself marginally satisfied with this kinder confession. He'd said as much before, but at least she understood why now.

"Or lack thereof," he told her, flashing that endearingly crooked smile. "I can't control myself." He gestured wearily. "You saw what happened this afternoon. I burned a tenderloin, then had to kiss you because it was your fault."

Carrie's eyes widened. "My fault?"

His gaze met hers over the rim of his wine glass. "Yes, of course."

Oh, this should be good. She grinned. "And how was *your* burning the tenderloin *my* fault?"

"I was distracted," he explained patiently, as though she were a half-wit. "By your breasts."

Carrie cocked her head and smiled. "Back to those, are we?"

He muttered something which sounded suspiciously like, "I wish."

She shot him a look, then stood. "Do you mind if I work while we talk?" she asked, thinking that a change of subject was in order.

Before she did something stupid, like lean forward and kiss him again. Or remove her shirt so that they would pick up exactly where they'd left off this afternoon.

Philip swiftly swallowed the drink in his mouth, set his wineglass aside and hurriedly stood. "Better still, how about I help you?"

Carrie darted a droll look at him over her shoulder. "Oh, I don't know. I'd hate for you to get *distracted*."

Philip's eyes crinkled, and he bit his bottom lip as his gaze instantly dropped to her chest. Her nipples tingled and an answering warmth burned in her sex. "I should be fine so long as you don't take off your shirt."

Carrie didn't know what made her do it—faulty reasoning, the inability to resist a dare, sexually induced insanity. Who knew? But one second she'd been standing there fully clothed and the next, she'd grabbed the hem of her shirt and slowly—deliberately—pulled it up and drew it over her head.

Then she dropped it. An improvised gauntlet, but judging from the smoky arousal in Philip's eyes and the slow crooked smile sliding across those magnificent lips, she'd done something right.

Two seconds later he was on her.

9

HE SHOULD HAVE KNOWN BETTER than to taunt her, Philip thought as he watched Carrie suddenly grow still. Watched that martial light spark in those gorgeous violet eyes. Then her hands found the hem of her shirt and well…

She pulled it off, let it drop purposely to the floor and he'd…come undone.

He'd registered bare belly, lacy push-up bra and creamy cleavage and the tenuous hold he'd had on reason and restraint had snapped like a fine twig beneath a bull elephant's hoof. Two steps across the room and she was warm and willing in his arms.

Two more and he had her against the refrigerator.

"You win," he said again, his voice strangled and barely recognizable to his own ears.

He felt Carrie smile beneath his kiss, her small hands slip beneath his shirt at the small of his back. "I win what?"

"Me," he chuckled, toeing his shoes off. He

kicked them across the room and from the corner of his eye saw Hoover's head pop up from his bed. "Aren't you lucky?"

She sucked his tongue into her mouth, then moved her hands around to the front of his shorts, ably finding the button. "Ask me in an hour," she said breathlessly, his zipper humming to her joke.

Another quick laugh caught him unaware. Granted he was good, but if she thought he had the stamina to last an hour when he seriously doubted his ability to take her without detonating upon entry, then she had more faith in him than he did.

"Wishful thinking, darling." He pushed her shorts and panties down her legs, felt her kick them aside, then drew back long enough to shrug out of his shirt and carelessly tossed it aside. Her bra fortuitously fastened in the front. A mere flick of his finger later, he'd popped the snaps, licked the valley between her cleavage and slung the bedamned thing aside. It caught the pot rack hanging from the ceiling.

A hiss stuttered between his teeth when his bare skin connected with hers. "I've wanted you too long." He laughed. "You've, uh, had me in knots since the first time I watched your show."

Carrie slipped her hands beneath his shorts and briefs, forcing them down his legs. Philip almost stumbled in his haste to get them off quickly enough.

Now, now, now, he thought, his brain firing the mantra in time with his frantic heartbeat.

A purr of pleasure vibrated up her throat as he circled the delicate shell of her ear with his tongue. She drew her hands up over his back, tunneled them into the hair at his nape, causing a rush of gooseflesh to break out over his arms. His eager dick nudged at her soft belly.

Christ. He'd be lucky if he didn't detonate *before* entry. She smelled like sugar and strawberries and hot, sweet sex and he wanted her more than he'd ever wanted anything in his life. To hell with his show. She could have it. He just wanted her. Right now. Against the freaking refrigerator.

"I could say the same about you," she said, thoroughly surprising him.

Philip drew back, felt a gratifying smile slide across his mouth. "You could?"

She leaned forward and licked the hollow of his throat. "I could. I've been watching you for *years*. Since before you came to New Orleans." She nipped lightly at his shoulder, causing his breath to stall in his lungs. "And I've been lusting just as long."

Philip lifted her up, felt her smooth legs wrap around his waist and his eager dick brush her hot, wet flesh. A shudder racked his body and he set his jaw so hard he feared it would crack. She gasped, rocked instinctively towards him.

Her kitchen, against a major appliance with her dog looking on, and he didn't give a damn.

He braced her back against the refrigerator, bent his head and pulled the crown of her sweet pink breast into his mouth. *Ah…heaven,* Philip thought as her taste blossomed across his tongue. He fed wildly at her, couldn't lick, suck or taste enough. Need hammered away inside his head, bludgeoning years of thoughtful lover training into oblivion. He didn't have the strength, the will, to do anything besides devour her.

Take her.

Carrie inhaled sharply, her hips involuntarily rocking forward once more, pushing him even farther between her drenched folds.

Then the most horrible thought occurred to him, one that he hadn't failed to consider since he started dipping his wick—he didn't have a condom. He held himself perfectly still and wretchedly confessed. If he had to stop now, he'd probably expire.

"I'm clean and covered," she said breathlessly, her eyes glazed with want. "Please tell me you are."

Philip pushed against her once more, felt relief melt every bone in his body except the one eagerly nudging between her hot legs. "Not to worry. I am."

"Oh, thank God. Philip," she pleaded, her voice a breathy plea. She bracketed his face with her hands, pulling his mouth up for another frantic kiss. Her tongue pushed into his mouth, thrust back and forth and his hips automatically caught that rhythm. Her wet sex rode the ridge of his erection and with every push he felt her body tightening, relaxing, then tightening again. Her breath came out in jagged little puffs and her skin dewed with sweat.

His thighs quaked and burned with the effort of restraint and when he feared he might collapse, he finally drew back enough to nudge her center. His vision blackened around the edges.

Carrie's sexy chuckle sounded in his ear. "Oh, thank God. I need— I want—"

Me, dammit, Philip, thought. *Say me.*

"—you," she finally said, a confession that touched him all the way to the core. With a primal growl which would have made his Cro-Magnon ancestors proud, he pushed into her, impaling her on his throbbing dick. Her breath caught, then eased out in a vastly relieved sigh.

Philip buried himself to the hilt, seating himself firmly between her thighs. If he'd ever experienced anything more perfect than the sensation of having Carrie locked around him, her feminine muscles clamping over him—*claiming him*—then he couldn't recall.

For the briefest of seconds between that first thrust and the second, in the smallest recesses of his mind, he recognized that something was different this time. Something significantly special had happened.

Then she'd leaned forward and nipped at his shoulder, tightened around him once more, and the sentiment was lost to sensation.

He just wanted her.

Philip grabbed her hips and pistoned into her, her soft pliant body eagerly absorbing his frantic thrusts. Her hands were everywhere—on his back, his neck, into his hair—impossibly enflaming him even more.

She mewled, gasped and swore and he felt her go rigid and melt…then go wild. "Oh, please," she cried, her fingernails biting into his back. "Philip, I—"

"I know," Philip all but growled. He could feel the tingle of beginning climax burning in his loins, knew he couldn't last much longer.

Her tight heat fisted around him and she met him thrust for thrust, forcing him to up the manic tempo. Impossibly the refrigerator rocked behind them and, perhaps it was merely his imagination, but he thought he could hear jars and cans wobbling around inside.

He didn't care. The whole damned house could come crumbling down around them and he wouldn't move from between her legs until she came, until every last spasm of pleasure had been milked from her magnificent body.

Just when he was certain that he wasn't going to be able to hold out—that he wasn't going to be able to make it happen for her before he came apart—she sang for him.

A sharp gasp, a desperate growl, every muscle in her body atrophied, she clamped hard against him, her head fell back against the refrigerator door and a soundless wail tore from her throat.

It was the most beautiful melody he'd ever heard.

And the most welcome because he thought he was surely going to die before he brought her to release.

Her wet heat fisted hard against him, evidently the secret code, because he suddenly came. Hard. Philip felt his lips peel back from his teeth. His legs weakened, his knees wobbled and it was all that he could do to keep them upright. The final pulses of her orgasm milked him of his—of the rest of his—strength and he slowly lowered her to the floor, then pressed a kiss against her forehead.

"You're amazing," Philip whispered, because the moment asked for it. Needed some sort of acknowledgment, even if it seemed horribly inadequate.

Carrie leaned forward and kissed his jaw. "You're not too bad yourself."

The idea of going home—of leaving her—and making the trip back across town to his big empty house made his stomach fill with a chilly horrid dread. He didn't want to be lonely…and knew he'd never be lonely with her.

Philip slid a finger reverently down the side of her face, then hesitated. "Can I spend the night?" he asked, for the first time since his childhood opening himself up for rejection.

A soft smile curled her lips. "Only if you'll carry me to bed," she said. "I'm not sure that I can walk."

Relief jimmied a sigh loose. "Well," he said, promptly gathering her up in his arms. "I was rather hoping you'd carry me. After all, I did all the work."

Carrie gasped and shot him an outraged look. "You did all the work?"

"Didn't I?" he asked innocently. Philip retraced his steps through the dining room, back to the living room and toward the staircase. "Is this the way to your bedroom?"

"No," she said, an odd light gleaming in those sleepy violet eyes. "It's at the back of the house."

Philip paused, slightly embarrassed that he'd hauled her in the wrong direction. Sort of ruined his gallant gesture. He should have asked. Served him right.

He retraced his steps, went back to the kitchen and looked for an entrance to her bedroom. He saw the back door, what was obviously a pantry and wash-room, but nothing which remotely resembled her sleeping quarters.

An odd suspicion rose and his gaze slid to hers. Her eyes sparkled with humor and her lips twitched at the corners. She looked completely comfortable wrapped up in his arms. Relaxed, and unlike him, not the least bit out of breath.

He felt his eyes narrow. "Your bedroom is up-stairs, isn't it?"

She laughed, the she-devil. "It is."

"Then why—"

"*You* did all the work?" she asked with a signifi-cant lift her brow.

Philip turned and made his way back through from whence he'd come, then headed up the stairs. He chewed the inside of his cheek. "That might have been a small exaggeration," he conceded.

He reached the landing and realized the upstairs

was a lot larger than what he would have thought. A wide hall bisected the middle and six doors—three on each side—loomed in front of him.

Carrie chuckled, sensing his dilemma. "Only a small one?"

"Which one is your room?" Philip asked, rather than going in and out of the wrong doors.

"I'll let you know when you go in it."

Since he'd rather get her into bed than belabor the point, Philip bit his tongue and smiled. "Okay," he relented. "It's quite possible that you did *some* of the work."

"Thank you," she replied with a prim nod of her head, evidently pleased with his reluctant concession.

"Now which one is yours?"

"Third door on the right."

"Excellent," Philip said, and headed in that direction. "But I still did *most* of the work."

Carrie gasped and punched him lightly on the arm as he finally strolled into her bedroom. "Fine," she said. "I suppose that you think I should make it up to you?"

He gently deposited her on the bed, watched her hair fan out over her pillow. A startling combination of affection and need broadsided him, forcing him to set a knee against the mattress.

Philip cleared his throat. "Making it up to me sounds like a fine plan," he managed.

Smiling, Carrie tugged him toward her. "You win," she said.

Philip felt a laugh break up in his throat. "Win what?"

She rolled him onto his back, then straddled him. Her eyes twinkled with humor and were sleepy with want. "Me."

God help him, Philip thought.

10

IF SHE COULD SET THE SCENE any more perfectly, Etta James's "At Last" would be drifting softly through the room and a steady rain would be pouring down outside, punctuated by the occasional rumble of thunder.

Instead, they'd showered together in lieu of rain— a blessedly sensual pastime which involved lots of shower gel and a mental thank-you to the contractor who'd firmly secured the metal shower ring to the ceiling above her claw-foot tub. It was the first time she'd ever had occasion to practically hang from it, Carrie thought with a slow smile. As for the storm, Hoover's dubious grumbling from the floor beside the bed doubled for thunder.

But she had managed to make one part of her fantasy with Philip become a reality. Carrie tipped the black truffle oil nozzle onto her finger, got just a little—waste not, want not, after all—then painted his nipples with the heady, fragrant oil.

Laying flat on his back, hands laced behind his head, he epitomized sexy and relaxed as candlelight illuminated the fascinating landscape of his smooth, muscular body.

Living art, Carrie thought with a quiet needy sigh.

His broody silver eyes watched her carefully and a faintly wicked smile caught the corner of his mouth. "Why do I get the feeling that this is something you've given quite a bit of thought to?"

Carrie bent her head and lapped at him, sighing with pleasure as the pungent taste hit her tongue. "Because I have," she murmured huskily. "It's all part and parcel of my wild-gorilla-sex-with-Philip-on-a-dark-and-stormy-night-with-truffle-oil fantasy."

His head tipped back, allowing a deep chuckle to vibrate up his masculine throat. "Well, I think we covered the wild gorilla sex part in the kitchen, you've got the truffle oil and it's dark, but I'm afraid stormy wasn't in tonight's forecast."

Odd, then, Carrie thought, because when he'd pushed into her downstairs tonight, she'd felt like she'd been hit by lightning.

Positively electrified.

Every hair on her body had stood on end from the shock of his hot invasion. Every cell had peaked, her skin had prickled, and every molecule which made up her quivering form had sung with that bizarre, impossible recognition.

Her body *knew* him, craved him, needed him.

Had she not been on the brink of orgasm from the instant she touched him, she would have been terrified. As it was, she hadn't had time to be terrified.

She'd merely *felt*.

And it had been amazing.

Carrie had wanted him—there had never been any question about that. She'd fantasized, dreamed and longed for Philip since the first time she'd caught sight of that crooked smile on her television screen. She'd wanted to taste, treasure, and touch every inch of his body.

She'd wanted to cook with him, curl up on opposite ends of the couch and read a book with him. She wanted to talk politics and religion with him—the sticky subjects which revealed more than a person's opinion but a measure of their character.

She wanted to know the names of the pets he'd had as a child, an explanation for every scar on his body. She wanted to know if he'd been popular or shy, when he'd lost his virginity and to whom. Had his interest in cooking come from a family member or, like her, was there a deeper meaning behind her desire?

To put it simply, she wanted to know everything about him. Every last niggling detail.

Her gaze slid over his chest, down his belly and rested at the long hardened length of him jutting proudly toward his navel. Carrie snagged her oil once more and let go a shuddering breath of anticipation.

But first things first…and admittedly, her fantasy was a priority.

She loaded her finger once more and drew a line down his ridged belly, into his navel, then further south until she reached her ultimate destination. He jumped eagerly into her hand, warm and thrilling, hard and ready.

Philip hissed with pleasure and his thighs tensed. "Carrie," he said warningly.

"Shhh. I'm doing something."

A choked laugh broke up his throat. "I know that. It's *what* you're doing that's killing me."

Then prepare to die, Carrie thought with a wicked chuckle. She flipped her hair out of the way, swirled her oiled finger around his engorged tip, then bent and slowly licked it off.

"Sweet mother of— *Carrie*." Philip's hands fisted in her sheets.

She smiled, then took the whole of him into her greedy mouth. The taste of warmed black truffle oil and musky man tantalized her tongue, hypnotized her senses. He was smooth and hard and he felt like living velvet in her mouth. Carrie worked the base of him with her hand, chased it with her mouth and tongue, up and down, making a feast of him. She moaned in pleasure against him, wanted him to know just how much she enjoyed him, how much she relished feeling him in her mouth.

Honestly, she could get addicted. There was something so hedonistic about being with him. He lit every sense, heightened every feeling.

Apparently unable to withstand her single-siege against him, Philip's hands were suddenly on her, rolling her onto her side. In the blink of an eye, he realigned their bodies, hooked her thigh around his shoulder, then parted her curls and lapped at her weeping flesh.

The first shock of contact—his facile tongue against her pulsing clit—made the air rush out of her lungs in a startled broken exhalation.

"Mmm," he moaned. "Why should you be the only one to get fed?"

Carrie licked the underside of his penis, sucked at the sensitive skin. "Funny. I was thinking, why did I have to do all the work?"

His chuckle echoed against her and he parlayed the taunt by slipping his finger deep inside her, then upping the tempo against her tender nub. "I know exactly what you mean," he told her, the wretch.

She felt her muscles clamp against him, felt the first sparkler of impending climax light deep in her womb. Oh, no, Carrie thought, upping her ministrations, he wasn't doing this to her. The next time she came she wanted to be on top of him, riding out the climax above his magnificent body.

That had been her fantasy, after all.

Carrie tongued him a few more times, simply because she couldn't resist. He was like a chocolate kiss or a potato chip. One taste was never enough. Another tight flash of tingling heat engulfed her sex, forcing her to rethink her current position.

This was nice…but him being inside her would be better.

She gave him another slow, tender pull, then gently untangled herself from him long enough to roll him onto his back. She scaled his body, settled herself above his hard sex and winced with pleasure as his smooth head bumped her swollen clit.

"Carrie," he said warningly again.

Like she was actually going to listen to him? she thought, smiling. What was he going to do? Stop her? She had him right where she wanted him—where she'd needed him for the past year—firmly beneath her thighs.

She bent forward, purposely raking the tips of her breasts against his chest, and licked the side of his neck. His masculine hair abraded her needy nipples, sending another lightning bolt of electricity through her.

"Holy..." he choked out.

Carrie chuckled, slid over him once more, coating his rigid length with her feminine juices. "We're getting there," she said.

Philip's big wonderful hands moved over her back, spanned her waist, then molded to her rump, causing her belly to shudder with a broken breath. "Not soon enough. Bloody hell, Carrie. If you're going to— Would you please just—" Philip lifted his hips and pushed against her, desperately trying to get inside her.

Since she wanted that, too, she leaned back, raised her rump and slowly, painstakingly lowered herself onto him. The sensation was exquisite.

Timeless.

Her lungs deflated with each increment of his hot welcome invasion into her body and by the time she'd fully seated herself on top of him, she was in serious danger of passing out. An involuntary thing like *breathing* was suddenly beyond her. Every thought, every sensation, every ounce of her energy was invested in what was happening below her waist, at their joined bodies.

Philip looked up and those heavy-lidded pewter eyes tangled with hers. The emotion she saw there—the stark need—made something in her chest swell and fracture. Something extremely significant had just happened, hovered right out of her immediate understanding, but she let it drift away, too caught up in him to heed it.

Philip growled low in his throat, pushed up again and her feminine muscles instinctively tightened around him. She lifted herself up, dragging the tension out, savoring the erotic friction between them. He filled her so completely she could feel every pulse, every ridge and vein deep inside her.

He tightened his hold on her hips, then leaned forward and dragged the crown of her breast deep into his mouth, unwittingly causing an answering tug in her muddled womb. Carrie's breath hitched in her throat and she rode him harder.

Up, down, up and down. Philip suckled her harder, seemed to sense the exact instant to lick and tug, to thrust and hold back. He was reading her, Carrie realized, impressed. She subjected him to similar scrutiny, watched his face for every flickering lash and wince of pleasure. Listened to those intensely sexual sounds—a keening growl of approval, a restless grunt of satisfaction, then corroborated those telling gestures with the appropriate action.

He dug his heels into the mattress, veins appeared in his arched neck and a long guttural howl tore from his throat. A hot flash of heat bathed the back of her womb as his climax tore through him and rocketed into her.

As though his somehow tripped a hidden trigger, Carrie's own orgasm crested and broke through her. A soundless keening shriek rose in the back of her throat and she threw her head back, channeling the sensation. Her feminine muscles clamped around him, each exquisite squeeze of her release sapping her strength as it tightened around his still-pulsing shaft.

When the last tremor subsided, she collapsed onto his chest, spent and boneless. The warm scent of hot sex, dark truffle oil and vanilla candles permeated the air. Her hair slithered over her shoulders, cascaded onto his side and pooled onto the mattress. His heart pounded against her cheek and his talented fingers drew lazy circles on her back. That nagging sense of homecoming and well-being blanketed her as her lids drooped.

Philip stirred beneath her. "Hey," he said softly.

"Mmm hmm."

"Do you hear that?"

Sleep tugged at her. "Hear what?"

"It's raining."

Carrie listened for the telltale sound against her slate roof and a soft smile curled her lips. "The total package," she murmured, then drifted off to sleep, safe, sated and warm in the perfect comfort of his arms.

PHILIP FELT Carrie's breathing level off into the rhythmic pattern of peaceful sleep. She lay snuggled against his side, her head pillowed on his chest, her small hand slightly curled but open in a curiously trusting gesture which somehow had the power to completely undo him.

Candlelight flickered across her face, played over the moonbeam waterfall of hair cascading over his chest and barely illuminated the pale green bottle of truffle oil she'd absently set on the bedside table. She'd tugged a sheet up until it barely covered her beautifully rounded rump, and the soft swell of her womanly frame lay outlined underneath.

Philip had slept with more women than he'd ever thought to count. He'd had sex in a train, on a bus, in an airplane, the bathroom of the Louvre, and in a small knot garden in a Benedictine abbey outside of Kent. He figured if the Almighty had struck him down on the spot for that, he had a fairly decent shot at making it into heaven.

He'd dated waitresses, attorneys, supermodels and salesclerks. Even twins and one unique set of Japanese triplets. He'd had extensive sexual experience with a variety of women and yet nothing in that vast repertoire could come close to what had just happened to him with Carrie.

The sex hadn't just been good—it had been... *phenomenal.*

There were no words to describe what he'd felt, the absolute rapture of perfection he'd experienced when he'd finally slid into her. It was as though his very organic makeup had shifted and changed, realigned and reassembled...and he'd come out better.

For the first half second inside her body, he'd been unable to breathe, cognitive thinking had ceased and he'd felt a quake in his chest that had made the fine hairs on the back of his neck stand on end. An overwhelming sense of peace and security had washed over him—of love, God help him, when he knew it wasn't possible—and he'd been hit with the strangest urge to laugh, then weep.

Weeping wasn't an option—it hadn't been since his sister had passed away. His parents had forbid it. Apparently they hadn't wanted a reminder of their own grief and, furthermore, the two of them had been so emotionally wasted after Penny died, he knew they didn't have it in them to comfort him. He'd just lost a little sister, a future friend. He smiled bitterly. Why would he need any comfort?

Philip shoved the unsettling memories aside, refused to let them taint what had been a singularly life-altering evening. At any rate, since weeping had been out of the question, he'd focused his energies on her.

On having her, specifically.

Philip had instinctively known that things would be different with her. Even when he'd been locked in the little padded cell of sexual insanity, he'd realized that she was special, that she was someone he could easily have feelings for. Hell, asking her if he could spend the night had been a huge leap for him. He wasn't accustomed to asking anyone for anything.

But the idea of going home when he could be with her... Well, it had been worth the risk.

She had been worth the risk.

So much for coming over here to apologize for kissing her and putting the brakes on their budding relationship, Philip thought, idly doodling figure-eights over her slim back. He'd spent the entire drive over here planning that very conversation, had planned to offer an olive branch to simply get through the rest of the week, and yet one look into those light-purple eyes and he'd completely forgotten his original agenda.

Ah, hell, Philip thought. He'd been grasping at straws to think it would work anyway. Snapping this afternoon and kissing her should have told him that. What sort of a moron thought "kissing" was the right sort of punishment for anything? What sort of twisted logic had brought him to that conclusion?

He'd just latched onto any reason to justify hauling her into his arms and that had been it. In the end, she could have been the world's most accommodating host and he would have kissed her anyway, simply because he couldn't *not* kiss her.

Which brought another potential—only one of many—to mind. Keeping his hands to himself tomorrow while they were on camera was going to be a serious exercise in restraint. Not that it hadn't been up until this point. His self-proclaimed CHiC—he still couldn't get over that, Philip thought with a fond smile—had been on a personal mission to make him sexually miserable via those skimpy outfits she wore.

Technically she'd been wearing them for him, but after tonight, he was relatively certain the sentiment behind the action would change significantly. Take on a whole new meaning. She would be more than the *Negligee Gourmet*—she'd be *his Negligee Gourmet*.

He rather liked the idea.

But what he didn't like was the idea of men all across America sitting in front of their TVs ogling her and whacking off. Hell, he'd done it. He knew what men were like. Bloody animals, the lot of them.

Oh, shit, Philip thought. He really wished he hadn't thought about that. Something entirely Neanderthal—like jealousy—was suddenly twisting his guts into helpless knots of he-man rage. Call him crazy, but he didn't want anyone looking at her. The only person who should be granted access to seeing her delectable breasts was him, dammit.

Something had to be done about this, Philip thought. Aside from the fact that he knew she hated wearing those outfits—intuition, of course—she deserved better than being treated like a damned sex object. She was so much more. Furthermore, with the exception of himself, there wasn't a single host employed by the network who had more talent. Carrie was a natural at all of it. She made it look easy.

Why had she agreed to it? Philip wondered again. What had made her sign that contract when he felt certain she could have held out and gotten a better deal? Funny how he'd had this odd connection to her from the beginning—that nagging sense of knowing her, recognizing her—and yet there were still so many things he didn't know about her.

He felt her stir against him, causing an inexplicable rush of tender emotion to wash through him. Her soft breath fanned against his chest and he looked down and caught sight of that sweet hand, the gentle shape of that plump, soft palm. Odd how he should find it so endearing. It was just a hand after all. Most everyone had them. And yet something about hers made his stomach clench with unwarranted affection.

Philip yawned, shifted her more snugly against him. A small crack of thunder rumbled in the distance and the soothing sound of rain tapped against the windows, lulling him in the quiet cozy comfort of her room. Would that he never had to go home, Philip thought sleepily. In her arms, he'd never…be lonely…again.

11

O<small>N LEGS THAT WERE STILL</small> a little shaky—quick, hot sex on the floor of a dressing room would do that to a person, she thought with a grin—Carrie hurried into Madame LeBeau's for her dress fitting. She was twenty minutes late, but since the seamstress could work on the other bridesmaids first, she didn't think it would be a big deal. A slow smile curled her lips.

She'd already had The Big Deal.

Philip had followed her into her dressing room when their show was over this morning—under the pretense of looking at tomorrow's breakdown again, of course—and had shut her door with a purpose that had sent a thrill whipping through her all the way down to her silver toe ring.

She wasn't the only one who got points for efficiency, Carrie thought as a smile bloomed around her heart. He'd unbuttoned his pants with one hand and, rather than waste time removing her panties, he'd simply nudged the slinky fabric to the side with the other. Mouths locked in a hot kiss, hands groping wildly, they'd half fallen onto her small couch, then ultimately tumbled to the floor.

Carrie hadn't cared.

There was something downright thrilling about a man who couldn't wait. Who wanted her so much that seduction and finesse became secondary to the attraction. She'd locked her legs around his waist, met him thrust for thrust, and by the time he'd collapsed on top of her, she'd had a hard, back-clawing orgasm, her hair had been in tangles and she was sporting carpet burns on the small of her back.

Despite the mild discomfort now, she'd do it again in a heartbeat. Getting through the show today after everything that had happened last night had been difficult to say the least. She couldn't look at him without mentally stripping him and recreating the truffle oil fantasy. The smallest crook of his mouth into that sexy little smile made her belly hot and muddled, made her organs practically vibrate. Undoubtedly she'd had a ridiculous smile on her face throughout their entire show…but she simply hadn't been able to contain herself.

For the first time in years, she'd was experiencing something which had been genuinely lacking in her life—happiness. Her friends made her happy, of course. But this was a different kind of joy—the romantic sort that seemed to make her vision brighter and clearer. Made her want to twirl around and sing *The Sound of Music* and listen to every circa 1980s big-hair-band ballad.

Curling up next to Philip last night, falling asleep to the steady rhythm of his heartbeat and the soft falling rain of a summer storm, his warm body next to hers had been a singularly fantastic experience. She couldn't imagine anything more perfect. The rest of the world had simply fallen away and she'd been safe in the cocoon of his curiously restful company.

And when he'd asked if he could spend the night, her silly heart had simply…melted. There'd been something so cautiously hopeful about his question, a hesitancy which told her that A.) he wasn't accustomed to asking for anything, and B.) at some point in his life he'd been hurt deeply. She'd caught a glimpse of some inner turmoil, a pain so old and stark that *she'd* felt it, too.

It was the haunted look of a wounded, lonely man, Carrie thought, wondering what had happened to put that sort of ache in his heart. Something—or someone—had made him vulnerable. She knew it. And she also knew that opening himself up to her last night had been a huge step for him.

And he'd taken it for her.

"Well, well, well," Frankie drawled, arms crossed

over her chest. "Is she not a walking picture of glowing sexual happiness or what?" her friend joked in a voice loaded with ooh-la-la innuendo.

Carrie's step faltered as she entered the back room of the upscale boutique and a smile broke out over her mouth. "Frankie," she admonished.

Presently standing on the dais having her dress altered, Zora gave Carrie a slightly critical look, then grinned. "As usual, you're right, Frankie. She's definitely got the Orgasm Aura."

Madame LeBeau smiled around a mouthful of pins and shook her head. "Oy. Young people." She glanced at Carrie. "You should put on your dress. I'll need you in a minute."

Eyes twinkling, April chuckled under her breath. "Well?" she prodded. "Are the sex sleuths correct? Did you and Philip finally—"

"—bump uglies?" Frankie supplied helpfully. "Do the horizontal mambo, play mattress Olympics, scr—"

"Ignore her," Zora said, shooting Frankie a fondly exasperated look. "Just give us an update."

"With *lots* of details," Frankie added, raising her brows significantly.

"After you put on the dress," Madame LeBeau said firmly, shooing her off. "Room four. It's on the hook and don't worry about zipping it up. I'll take care of it when you come back out."

Carrie hurriedly rushed to the back, quickly disrobed and shimmied into her gown. It was a beautiful sleeveless tea-length organdy in Victorian lilac. Frankie had chosen a gorgeous shade and timeless feminine style which would complement each bridesmaid's coloring and figure. Even the very pregnant one, Carrie thought with a wry smile.

"What's the holdup?" Carrie heard Madame LeBeau call in brisk carrying tones. "Does it not fit? Have you locked yourself in the dressing room?"

"I'm coming," Carrie told her, rolling her eyes. Honestly, she might be the most renowned dressmaker in the area, but the woman was an absolute pill.

Carrie met Zora in the hall. "Too bad New Orleans' Golden Needle has the personality of a pit bull," Zora whispered dryly as Carrie hurried past.

Madame LeBeau gestured for her to stand upon the dais. "Excellent," she said, eyeing the fit of Carrie's dress. "Very little alteration." She bent at the hem and started working.

"Well?" Frankie demanded again. "What happened?"

Carrie struggled not to grin. She should have known Frankie wasn't going to let it drop. She poked her tongue in her cheek and tried to think of the best way to sum up what had happened between her and Philip.

Various images from last night and this afternoon shot rapid-fire through her mind—her back against the refrigerator, Philip driving into her. Hanging from her shower rod—literally—her legs hooked over his shoulders while he fed at her. Male nipples and truffle oil, carpet burns and melting orgasms. Renewed heat muddled her womb and, embarrassingly, her nipples pearled beneath the thin fabric.

Naturally, gimlet-eyed Frankie who'd been not-so-patiently waiting for her to explain noticed. She stared pointedly at Carrie's breasts. A slow dawning smile slid across her face and she beamed at Carrie as though she were a difficult pupil who'd finally mastered her multiplication facts. "Never mind," she said. "I see evidence that you took our advice."

Carrie blushed. "Yes," she finally admitted. "I *like* cooking with something besides gas."

Struggling to flatten her smile, April cleared her throat. "And how was your meal?"

"My *meals* were outstanding." She resisted the urge to rock back on her heels. Somehow she didn't think Madame LeBeau would appreciate her moving around. "As were my appetizers, main courses, side dishes, desserts and after-dinner mints."

Zora waddled back into the room, paused and rubbed her back. An uncharacteristic wince marred her usually serene brow.

They'd all noticed, but April was the first to respond. "Zora? Are you okay?"

"Sure. It's just a little back pain. I have it all the time now."

Frankie studied her closely. "Are you having contractions?"

"They're Braxton-Hicks. They'll, uh... They'll go away soon."

Zora certainly sounded like she knew what she was talking about, Carrie thought, but she couldn't help but be concerned. Technically she wasn't due for another couple of weeks, but babies sometimes had their own timetables. "You're sure?" Carrie asked.

Zora nodded confidently, let go a breath and leaned against the arm of the couch. "I'm sure. It's just getting closer, that's all. Nothing to worry about."

Madame LeBeau, who'd been trying to pretend as if she wasn't hanging onto their every word, suddenly stood. "I'm done with you," she said. She turned to Frankie. "Everything will be ready on Friday. You can pick up your gowns then."

Still staring concernedly at Zora, Frankie nodded absently. "Okay."

"I'm fine," Zora insisted to Frankie. "Really. It's nothing to worry about."

Still looking somewhat unconvinced, Frankie finally nodded and let it drop. The four of them made their way out onto the sidewalk. After going over some last-minute details, April walked with Zora to her car, leaving Frankie and Carrie in front of the store.

Frankie watched Zora go, her brow still knotted in a worried frown. She plucked her cell from her purse. "I'm calling Tate anyway," she said. "He needs to keep an eye on her."

That sounded like an excellent plan, Carrie thought. Better safe than sorry, and she knew her friend well enough to know that she'd keep the incident from her husband. Zora always thought she knew what was best for everyone, but had a lamentable tendency to forget what was best for her.

"You look happy," Frankie said matter-of-factly, turning that shrewd gaze back in Carrie's direction.

Carrie bit her bottom lip, looked away and pushed her hair behind her ear. She nodded thoughtfully. "For the moment I am," she admitted.

Frankie cocked her head. "I've got a good feeling about this."

She hoped she was right, Carrie thought. She wasn't ready for his-and-her towels by any stretch of the imagination, but she had to admit there was a small tender sprout of hope lurking in her heart that Philip could be The One.

Speaking of which… Carrie glanced at her watch. "I've got to run."

Frankie arched a brow and a meaningful smile slid around her lips. "Plans?"

"As a matter of fact, yes. Philip's helping me with your cake tonight."

Frankie grinned and turned to go. "Do me a favor, would you?"

"Sure."

"Have your *appetizers, meals, side dishes, desserts and after-dinner mints* somewhere besides the kitchen. I'll take my cake sans sex, please," she quipped, then laughing, turned and made her way across the street.

Carrie chuckled. She'd have her cake and Philip, too, thank you very much.

"SEX IS EXCELLENT for your disposition," Rupert drawled with a smile that claimed responsibility for Philip's recent happiness. His agent currently leaned against the doorjamb of his master bath, watching him with a curiously speculative look. "You're in an excellent humor, better than I've seen you in more than a year. I take it *The Negligee Gourmet* was able to…cook up a remedy?"

Philip leaned forward and carefully ran a razor over his jaw. She'd certainly remedied something, he thought, remembering the exquisite perfection of her hot body clamping around his this morning after their show. Considering that he'd come dangerously close to bending her over the kitchen island while on camera, Philip thought he'd done a remarkable job exercising the restraint to wait until they'd finished taping.

Rather than wait around for Jerry and Joyce to go on and on about their "chemistry" and "heat" and "special spark," Carrie had calmly asked Philip if he'd look over tomorrow's breakdown, then the wench had shot him a saucy wink and he'd casually followed her all the way to her dressing room.

Then he'd snapped.

Much as he had before, when he'd flipped and kissed her. Only this time he knew what she would taste like, how fantastic she'd feel—how carnally responsive—and he hadn't been able to employ any sort of thoughtful seduction.

He'd freed his dick from his pants, scooched her panties over and toppled her like a randy virgin boy desperate to get at his first lover. He'd taken her with all the finesse of a sex-crazed bull elephant. Hell, he'd practically knocked her to the bloody floor, Philip thought, feeling his lips slip into a faint smile.

Thankfully, she didn't seem to mind.

And if anything, she'd seemed to enjoy it all the more. Last night when he'd finally fallen asleep with her, Philip hadn't given any thought to how they would work together today. Frankly, doing any sort of thinking last night had been out of the question. It had been too remarkable. Too…much, for lack of any better description.

Last night had been, simply put, *the* best night of his life.

Being with her had been… Philip paused, remembering. He let go an unsteady breath. It had been… unsurpassable. If he lived to be one hundred—no, forget that, Philip thought—if he lived *forever,* he knew he'd never have another evening so unbelievably perfect. Knew he'd never come close to finding the contentment he'd found in Carrie's arms. His gaze turned inward once more. Candlelight and moonbeam hair, that soft open palm.

Odd that of all the memories of last night, that was the one he kept coming back to. One would think he'd linger over visions of her breasts, plump and perfect, the soft curve of her hip, her sweet sex. Admittedly, those had revisited him. Philip swallowed.

But that darling hand upon his chest…that one had affected him.

Deeply.

In fact, for all intents and purposes, she might have well reached through his chest and touched his heart. For reasons he couldn't begin to fathom or explain, he knew it'd never be the same again.

If he had any sense at all he'd be terrified—he grimly suspected he knew what this feeling was, even if he wasn't ready to label it, and yet he lacked the emotional reserve to be frightened. He was too damned excited. Couldn't wait to get out of his house tonight and into hers.

"Much as I'm thrilled to see that you're enjoying yourself, we need to talk, Philip," Rupert said gravely.

Philip rinsed his razor and tapped it against the side of the sink. "About what?"

"Your performance with Carrie. You're having too much fun."

Philip chuckled. Now that was an understatement. Sexual tension aside, he loved working with her. They had an instinctive rhythm in the kitchen, could easily read each other, knew exactly how to segue into each segment of the show. In fact, neither one of them had even looked at the teleprompter today. They joked, laughed, had fun. They complemented each other extremely well and, though they'd only worked on three shows together, the camaraderie between the two of them bespoke of a much longer acquaintance.

"Having too much fun?" Philip asked. "Don't you think you're being a little paranoid, Rupert?"

"I'm not being paranoid," he snapped. "I'm being smart. I warned you yesterday that if you didn't dial things down a notch, I feared you were going to end up paired up with her permanently. I was under the impression that you were against that. Am I to assume now that your position has changed?"

"No," Philip said. Though, quite frankly, he wouldn't mind doing an *additional* show with Carrie, preferably fully clothed. Though he felt like a hypocrite—he'd certainly benefited from and enjoyed her half-dressed ensemble, particularly of late—he still thought that the marketing ploy cheapened her talent. She deserved better.

"Then, for your sake—and her feelings," he added, "I suggest that you not enjoy yourself quite so much these next couple of days. Both Joyce and Jerry have already called and asked for an audience Friday. It's not time to renegotiate. What, pray tell, could they want, I wonder?" Rupert paused, presumably to let that little morsel of news sink in.

Philip's instincts went on red alert. "They've both asked to see you?"

"Yes."

"Together or separate?"

"Together," Rupert said, confirming Philip's suspicions. Unless they were interested in lengthening the special or had some other idea in mind, there'd be no reason for the two of them to want to meet with Rupert together. Undoubtedly they had something up their sleeve…something that would most likely put him and Carrie at cross-purposes, which didn't bode well for their budding relationship.

"Shit," Philip swore. Why did things have to be so damned complicated? Why couldn't the network leave things well enough alone?

Rupert smiled grimly. "I thought you'd see things my way."

"I didn't say that."

Rupert shrugged. "You didn't have to."

Philip released an irritated breath. "What a bloody nightmare."

"Would you like me to get you a drink?"

"No, I'd like you to brush up on contract law. I think we're going to need it."

Oh, to hell with it, Philip thought, staring at his grave reflection in the mirror. He was worrying for nothing. He'd cooperated. He'd been a team player.

He'd done everything they'd asked him to do with the assurance from all parties that there was no ulterior motive.

Clearly, he was paranoid and worrying for nothing, and his own paranoia had rubbed off on Rupert. He wasn't going to think about it anymore. Refused to borrow trouble and ruin his relationship with Carrie. If they wanted to pair them up for good, he'd just say no.

Problem solved.

She'd understand, dammit. She might not like it, but she would respect his wishes. After all, he'd been up front with her. He'd never given her any reason to suspect that he'd like to make this co-hosting thing a permanent arrangement, right?

Satisfied that he'd argued himself out of a miserable corner, Philip nodded succinctly. Right.

Everything would be fine.

Starting with tonight…

12

PHILIP LEANED OVER her shoulder, his warm breath fanning against her neck causing a shower of goose bumps to race up her back. "That's excellent work," he murmured. "Beautiful detail."

Carrie sat her at her kitchen table, various tools and food-coloring paints lined up in front of her as she worked on Frankie's hummingbird. Actually painting the bird had ended up being a lot more difficult than making the form and sculpting it to start with. She'd contacted Ross this afternoon and gotten him to send a digital picture of the original stained glass ornament that she was basing her design on. It was her hope that Frankie would recognize it.

"Thank you," Carrie told him, carefully adding another stroke of color. She glanced across the table at the orange trumpet vine blossom Philip had done for her. "You don't do shabby work yourself."

Philip straightened. "Do you want me to work on the leaves now?" he asked.

Carrie paused long enough to look up. "Are you sure you don't mind?" She winced. "This is taking me longer than I thought it would."

Philip's sexy mouth curled into that crooked smile that made her breath hitch in her throat. "I don't mind at all. The sooner you get finished, the sooner we can move onto…other things," he said, his voice a slightly rough suggestive purr.

Carrie chuckled softly, cocked her head and released a small sigh. "So long as your motives are clear."

"I could make them very plain for you," Philip offered accommodatingly. He took the chair opposite her and set to work.

"Oh, I think they're plain enough."

He nodded, his lips twitching with the effort not to smile. "Just so there's no misunderstanding."

He was incorrigible, Carrie thought, and for some reason found that absolutely adorable. Tonight he wore another cool linen shirt—French blue, a fantastic shade for him—and a pair of loose white shorts. Pricey sandals were strapped onto his distinctly masculine feet. Carrie bit her lip, felt a hot flash of desire hit the tops of her thighs. He epitomized the perfect urban male, she decided—comfortably chic. Very sexy.

Though he hadn't looked at her, his eyes widened significantly. "If you want me to work for you, you've got to stop looking at me like that," Philip warned amiably. "I'm only a man. And a very horny one to boot," he added grimly.

"Sorry," Carrie said, making a concerted effort to not provoke him. She did appreciate the help, after all.

A comfortable silence stretched between them as they worked and there was something completely natural and right about Philip being here, in her kitchen, helping her. She felt as if they were part of a team, a cozy companionship that she instinctively knew she could become seriously addicted to. Hoover seemed to approve too, she thought, casting a fond look at her dog. He'd dragged his bed over next to Philip's chair and, after Philip had obligingly petted him, he'd lain down and gone to sleep.

"Tell me about England," Carrie said, deciding that a little personal information was in order.

Philip's gaze darted to hers and he arched a questioning brow. "You've never been before?" he asked.

Carrie shook her head.

"Odd," Philip remarked. "As much as you've

talked about traveling with your parents—Doctors Without Borders, right?—I just assumed…"

Carrie felt a little bud of pleasure unfurl in her chest. Had he actually watched every show? she wondered. "Too rich," she explained. "People with money don't need health care."

He carefully veined a small leaf. "Right. And where are your parents now?"

"Cambodia. Along with my brother. He's a doctor as well."

Philip looked up and frowned. "I don't think I've ever heard you mention him."

Carrie's lips quirked with droll humor as she painted the last bit of the first wing. She studied her handiwork critically, then corrected a slight mistake. "You must have missed that episode."

"Wrong," Philip told her. "I've seen them all. In fact, I have recorded every one of them."

Carrie grinned. "Is that right?"

"It is. Now back to the subject of your brother. Younger or older?"

She let go a sigh, dipped her brush and set to work on the other side. "Younger."

"And you weren't interested in being a doctor as well? No calling to go into the medical field?"

Carrie laughed. "Er…no. I can't stand the sight of blood."

Philip smiled at her. "Yes, well, I can see where that would put you at a disadvantage." He paused. "So why cooking? What led you in that direction?"

"I could ask the same of you," she said, wondering how her plan to carefully interrogate him for little morsels of information had suddenly been turned around on her.

"You certainly can," Philip said. "Later. Come on. Why cooking?"

If he was expecting her to confess to some grandiose dream of always having a passion for the art, then he was going to be sadly disappointed. It had come, but… "Believe me, there's nothing romantic about it."

"I don't care. What? Did you have a doting grandmother who baked with you? Fond memories of making cookies with your mother as a child?"

Carrie laughed. "Sorry. None of the above. I was an overweight child with serious food issues which were only compounded when we briefly came back to the States in my late teens. In order to beat it, I had to master it." She shrugged. "Becoming a chef was the product of that psychosis," she told him.

Now this was a first, Carrie thought as Philip goggled at her. She'd shocked him. "What?" she asked.

He shook his head, apparently trying to clear it.

"I'm sorry," he told her. "It's just so hard to imagine you being anything but perfect. You're beau—"

"I'm not perfect," Carrie said, unable to suppress the slight irritation in her voice. "Nobody's perfect. Being pretty doesn't make someone perfect. It doesn't make their life easier."

His smile slowly fell and he studied her closely. Dammit, Carrie thought. Why hadn't she just kept her mouth shut?

"I never said it did," Philip told her. "Sorry if I hit a button."

Irritated with herself, Carrie frowned and shook her head. "No apology needed. I overreacted. It's my hang-up, not yours." She paused, deciding she owed him an explanation for her outburst. "It's just, I know what it feels like to be imperfect. To be different. I lived with the stigma of being overweight. I was sneered at and ridiculed. Then I lost the weight and have lived with the stigma of being pretty." She gestured impatiently. "There's this perception that if you're thin and pretty, the world is your oyster…and frankly, that's a crock." She laughed bitterly under her breath. "I worked for Martin Renauld for years and there wasn't a day that went by when he didn't make some sort of snide comment. But I went in there every day and did my job because his was the best restaurant in town. When *The Negligee Gour-*

met deal came along, I'll be honest. I was disappointed. I thought I was getting a show where my talent was the selling point. I was wrong. My sex appeal was the selling point. My looks. I worried about selling out, about compromising, but in the end I did what was best for me and followed the money. Do I wish things were different? Yes. But they're still better and that's what I have to think about."

Seemingly digesting everything she'd said, Philip merely nodded. "Wow," he finally said. "I had no idea. I, er… I don't know what to say."

Curiously relieved that she'd explained herself, that she'd essentially laid all of her cards out on the table, Carrie smiled and shrugged. "You don't have to say anything. We're changing the subject anyway."

"We are? To what?"

"You. I've answered all of your questions—and then some," she said, poking her tongue in her cheek. "Now it's your turn."

Philip exhaled a weary breath. "I suppose you're right."

Carrie snagged a notepad and pretended to jot something down.

"What are you doing?" Philip wanted to know.

"You're right," Carrie said slowly, scrawling the words with a ridiculous amount of attention onto the paper. She finished and slid it to him. "Sign and date it please. I doubt I'll ever hear those words again."

Philip's eyes widened when he realized what she'd done and he laughingly pushed the pad back at her. "Sorry. I won't arm you with proof of your intelligence. You're too damned smart as it is."

Now, *that* was a compliment, Carrie thought, pleased. "Okay," she said. "What do I want to know first? Ah, yes. How old are you?"

He regarded her moodily. "Thirty-three."

"And where did you grow up?"

"Fulham, a suburb just inside London."

Carrie worked on her hummingbird's beak. "And have you been able to visit much since you moved here?"

"Visit who?" Philip asked. "My family's dead."

Had she not been concentrating, she would have fumbled her bird. She glanced up in time to see Philip wince, to see a flash of pain pass quickly over his features. He might have made a glib announcement, but there was clearly nothing glib about the pain it had caused him. The pain he still felt.

"I'm sorry," she said, stunned. "I had no idea."

Philip shook his head. "No worries. They've been gone a long time. Besides, you had no way of knowing."

Still. She felt like a moron and her heart broke for him. "What happened?"

"My mum had breast cancer." Philip swallowed. "Dreadful disease. She passed away four years ago. My, uh… My father couldn't deal with it. He committed suicide a week after we buried her."

"Oh, Philip," Carrie said, aching for him. How terrible. "I'm so sorry."

Philip didn't look up, but continued to work on the vines and leaves for the cake. "You know, this is going to sound harsh, but we weren't really all that close. My little sister drowned when she was five and they never quite recovered. They were so afraid that something might happen to me that they sort of, I don't know, disconnected I guess. As a result, I was never really able to get close to them." He let go a breath. "It was all for the best, I suppose, since they came to such a tragic end."

Losing one's entire family could not be for the best, Carrie thought, swallowing the lump of mournful outrage which had formed in her throat. "Your sister, what was her name?"

A fond smile drifted over his lips. "Penny. She had a head full of bright coppery hair. Thus her namesake."

Carrie continued to work, instinctively knew that Philip would shut down if he in any way suspected how this conversation was affecting her. Furthermore, she knew he wouldn't appreciate her pity. "And how old were you when she died?"

"Nine."

So old enough to remember being loved properly, but young enough to suffer years of lonely loss. That would certainly account for the haunting pain she'd seen in those gorgeous silvery eyes, Carrie thought. No wonder he guarded his heart so fiercely. He'd had to protect it because he was the only one who'd given a damn about it.

Until now, Carrie thought, feeling emotion seep into every swiftly thawing crevice of her heart. She gave a damn. In fact, were she completely honest with herself, she gave more than a damn.

Though reason told her that it was impossible— hell, they barely knew each other—instinct told her otherwise. She'd had that continual sense of familiarity since before meeting him and that feeling had been on fast-forward since Saturday.

Philip Mallory made her heart sing with recognition, her body resonate with pleasure and her soul hum with joy.

He was the yin to her yang, her missing part.

Carrie swallowed, traced the smooth line of his cheek with her gaze, silently watched him work and a rush of emotion engulfed her, made her heart squeeze painfully in her chest.

He completed her, Carrie thought, struggling to keep her composure. He made her whole.

"What?" Philip asked as though her world had not just tilted on its axis. "No more questions?"

Carrie painted the second eye on her humming-bird and gently set it aside. "Just one," she said.

Philip didn't look up, merely smiled one of those it-figured sort of grins. "Oh? What's that?"

"When are you taking me to bed?"

He stilled, then carefully looked up. His gaze tangled with hers, sucking all the air out of her lungs. Those silvery eyes suddenly glinted with molten heat. "Tell you what," he said thoughtfully. He paused, finished the bud he'd been working on, and placed it on the parchment paper. "How about I practice some of your notorious efficiency and take you now?"

A thrill shot through her, triggering a wicked giggle. "Now works for me."

HIS GUTS STILL CHURNING from that miserable conversation about his family, Philip abandoned any pretense of control, stalked around the table, pulled her from her chair up against his body, pushed his hands into that streaming moonbeam hair and staked a claim on her mouth that he hoped she'd never forget.

He poured every ounce of heartache and joy, misery and happiness into the meeting of their mouths. He gave it all to her, held nothing back. He couldn't. She'd laid him bare, had made him tell all—bloody share it all—and now she had to deal with the fallout. He wouldn't be denied. Wouldn't be ignored. Wouldn't simply cease to exist just to make things easier for her.

Carrie groaned into his mouth and he savored that sound, felt it reverberate against his tongue. "God, I want you," she said. She cupped his face in her hands, a tender yet erotic gesture that somehow had the power to make him want to alternately scream and weep. "I can't help myself. I just look at you and something happens to me. I melt," she said, slowly running her tongue across his bottom lip.

Philip's dick jerked against his shorts. He gathered her up, headed toward the door. "Is there a bedroom down here?" he asked. He didn't want to take the time to go upstairs. He wanted her now. Knew that the second he planted himself between her thighs the pain and smothering loneliness would abate and, for the moment, at any rate, he'd feel good. Whole.

As if he'd been born again and this time had come

out right. That he could be lovable no matter what happened. That someone couldn't simply *decide* not to care about him anymore. That wasn't love, dammit. Love was uncontrollable, wasn't a choice. It was felt, not doled out to only those one wanted to give it to.

"Who needs a bed?" Carrie said, licking a hot path up the side of his neck. Her teeth nipped at his earlobe, then her tongue pushed into his ear and he nearly dropped her it felt so damned good. A quake rocketed through him.

"You're right," Philip told her, swiftly changing directions. He settled her onto her kitchen counter. "Does this work for you?"

Carrie tore his shirt up over his head and slung it aside. "It will when you're inside me. Efficiency, Philip," she needled with a soft wicked chuckle. "Remember?"

Christ. She was going to be the death of him. She ran her hands over his bare chest, her face a mask of sleepy, greedy pleasure as her palms slid over him. "Talk about beautiful," she murmured.

Philip worked her skirt up her legs and stilled when his hands continued to find bare flesh. A choked laugh tore from his throat. "No panties?"

Carrie palmed him through his shorts, licked her lips, then swiftly opened his fly. "I thought I'd make things easier for you. FYI, I'm not wearing a bra either." He sprang free, right into her waiting hand. Her lids fluttered shut as she closed her fingers around him, causing a bead of moisture to ooze from his tip.

Philip pushed the straps of her tank top off her shoulders, slid it down until he'd bared both of her breasts. A mere nod of his head and she was in his mouth, pebbling against his tongue.

Carrie gasped, scooted forward and guided him to her center. "Come in," she pleaded. "Come inside me. Let me love you."

Let me love you.

He almost staggered. Philip braced both hands on the counter on either side of her, then pushed himself home. A combined sense of peace and chaos bombarded him, forcing him to lock his knees.

A storm of emotion and sensation tore through him, whipped his insides into a swirling mass of tender sentiment and the hot, driving need to brand her somehow. Make her permanently his. To be where no man aside from himself would ever be welcome again. The ache in his heart eased and a fractured laugh of relief shattered out of him, then she clamped around him, ran those sweet hands over his chest again and Philip simply let go. Let instinct take over.

When the last vestiges of release pulsed through them, Carrie reverently kissed his lids, his jaw, where neck met shoulder, then bent forward and tenderly kissed his chest, the region just above his still-racing heart.

And with that selfless gesture, he gave it to her.

13

"AND THAT CONCLUDES our *Summer Sizzling* special," Philip said, smiling at the camera.

Feeling decidedly wicked, Carrie lifted her foot and ran it up the side of Philip's leg. From the corner of her eye she watched his smile freeze. "We hope that you've enjoyed this week with us and that you've cooked up a little more than good food," she said with a significant lift of her brow. "Until then, best wishes for your *hot* dishes."

Jerry called it a wrap and the studio erupted in cheers. Rather than join in the festivities, eyes twinkling, Philip shot her a murderous smile. "I can't believe you did that," he said. "What if I'd dropped the plate?"

"But you didn't," she pointed out.

"But I could have."

"Disaster averted, eh? Besides, I was simply paying you back. I could have lopped a finger off when you copped a feel in Act Two."

He paused, remembering, then smiled unrepentantly. "Well, there is that."

Unable to help herself, Carrie chuckled. "I've had a good time with you this week," she said, feeling slightly sad that their working time together was over. At least, professionally, at any rate.

Though they'd spent every waking and non-waking moment together for the past couple of days, Carrie had purposely avoided the subject. Furthermore, she suspected he had, too.

Philip looked away, then that woefully familiar gaze found hers once more and a reassuring smile tugged at the corner of his curiously endearing mouth. "I have, too, Carrie. And I mean that. I know I was a bit of an ass—"

She cleared her throat loudly.

"Okay," he amended. "A complete ass about it in the beginning. But, extracurricular activities aside, it's been a pleasure. Seriously. You are a spectacularly fine chef and an equally fine host. I hope the network wises up and gives you the show you really deserve."

Warmed by his praise and sincerity, Carrie grinned and decided a little teasing was in order to lighten the moment. "So long as it's not yours, right?"

His eyes widened and a startled chuckle rumbled

from his chest. "Quite right. I'd prefer to keep my own."

"Completely understandable."

For whatever reason, he looked curiously relieved.

"Philip, Carrie," Joyce called above the small din. "The director wants to see you before you leave."

An unsettling sense of foreboding slipped up Carrie's spine. Philip's expression turned grim and they shared a look. If the director of programming wanted to see them—now, of all times—then that could only mean one thing: they wanted to change the format.

Philip swore under his breath, then grabbed her elbow and propelled her toward her dressing room. "Change first," he said. "Cleavage might help your cause, but pants will lend credibility."

Carrie scowled. She knew he was right, but found herself slightly annoyed at his high-handed tone nonetheless. "I'm quite capable of taking care of myself," she said tightly.

Looking like he was preparing for a rectal exam, Philip leaned against the wall and crossed his arms over his chest. "I'll wait here."

Carrie knew this had been his fear from the beginning—that he'd somehow get shunted out of his own show and permanently paired up with her—which was why she took deep calming breaths in an effort to cool her increasingly warming temper. How many times did she have to tell him that she didn't want his damned show? How many other ways could she say it?

She made quick work of changing her clothes and rejoined him in the hall. The silent trek up to the director's office was excruciatingly tense. Philip didn't say a word, merely scowled.

Dennis Spencer stood when they entered his office and greeted them with a warm smile. "Carrie, Philip," he said to each in turn. He gestured toward the tufted chairs positioned in front of his desk. "Please sit."

Philip looked as if he'd wanted to argue, but ultimately settled into the chair next to her. He nodded, acknowledging the director. "Spencer," he said tightly.

If Dennis was at all aware of Philip's displeasure—and he had to be because Carrie wasn't even looking at him and could feel the sentiment rolling off him in waves—then he did an impeccable job of not letting on.

"As I'm sure you're aware, the *Summer Sizzling* programming was my idea."

Carrie nodded, feeling her belly tip in a nauseated roll. Oh, hell. This couldn't be good.

"As I'm sure your producers have mentioned to

you, it's been a smashing success. We've received calls, e-mail and fan mail by the droves." He smiled encouragingly, as though they should be happy about this news.

Clearly, Philip wasn't.

Dennis's smile faltered, but he ultimately pressed on. "Apart, the two of you are fantastic. Together, you're *phenomenal*."

Philip's jaw hardened and he shifted forward in his chair. "Look, Spencer, I can see where you're going with this. As I'm sure you're aware, I didn't want to do this special to start with. I only came on board to prevent being in breach of contract."

Carrie had figured as much, but for some incomprehensible reason, hearing him say it pricked at her heart. It wasn't personal, she knew—at least not in the derogatory sense—but that didn't keep her from inwardly flinching all the same.

Dennis seemed to be weighing his options. His brow drew into a faintly thoughtful line and his shrewd gaze bounced between them. "I can see that trying to coax you into cooperating isn't going to work. So I'll just cut to the chase." His gaze found Carrie's. "Carrie, do you have any problem working with Philip?"

"No, but—"

"That'll do," he said, interrupting her. "Philip,

you've got another three years on your current contract. Without buying you out—which we have no intention of doing, by the way—there's nothing I can technically do to force your cooperation." He pulled a shrug. "I could continue organizing specials and putting you with Carrie...but we've got something a lot more permanent in mind."

Philip laughed bitterly. "Bloody hell," he said, then shot Carrie a look. "This is precisely why I didn't want to do this. I *knew* this would happen." He chuckled darkly. "It's my lot in life apparently."

Dennis ignored Philip's sarcasm and his gaze drifted to her. "Carrie, you on the other hand are due for renewal the end of the month."

Carrie swallowed, feeling distinctly sick. She'd known that, but other than instructing her agent to try to work on a better wardrobe, she hadn't really given much thought to it. "I'm aware of that," she finally said, for lack of anything better.

He smiled, but the action lacked genuine warmth. "Here's our position," he said, steepling his fingers beneath his chin. "Unless Philip agrees to join you on your show, then we're not going to renew your contract."

Carrie inhaled sharply and Philip vaulted from his chair. "You have got to be kidding," Philip snapped. "What's one got to do with the other? She's got excellent ratings in her own right! She's the best damned chef here!"

Looking extremely smug, Dennis leaned back in his chair. "Yes, well, I'm sure she hopes that you keep those things in mind when you make your decision."

Nausea clawed its way up the back of Carrie's throat and her head felt like it was going to explode. This could not be happening. It was simply too horrible to—

Philip braced both hands on the desk and leaned forward threateningly. "Here's the thing. I made my decision before we ever had this meeting. It's no."

Dennis looked genuinely surprised, but Carrie wasn't. Furthermore, she didn't blame him. "Philip," she began. "I—"

"Sorry, Carrie," he said in a voice that chilled her. "I can't do this. It's a deal breaker, if you know what I mean."

Then without another word, he turned and walked out.

If you know what I mean.

Significant ominous words, and unfortunately, she *did* know what they meant.

It was over.

He'd certainly ended that efficiently, hadn't he?

Carrie thought as her heart, true to form, just as efficiently broke.

"Look, Rupert," Philip barked into his cell phone. "I don't give a damn what you're doing or who you're doing it to or for. You get over here and take care of this mess now, or I swear this time I'll really fire you."

That sanctimonious little pissant, Philip thought, his mind a black hole of rage as he stormed out of the studio to his car. Who would have ever thought Dennis Spencer had it in him to be such a—

"What are you raving about?" Rupert said. "Slow down and start over."

Philip related Spencer's threat once again, felt his blood pressure gathering vein-bursting strength. "Can he do that?" Philip demanded. "Can he simply choose to not renew her contract if I don't agree to work with her?"

Rupert's sigh sounded through the line. "Yes, I'm afraid he can. Look, Philip, I know that you're upset, but this is really an issue that her agent needs to address, not yours."

Philip slid behind the wheel, started the engine and shot out of the parking garage. "But there has to be something I can do," he argued. "I don't want her getting fired on my account."

"Do you want to work with her?"

Philip negotiated traffic, did a mental search of his fractured thoughts and tried to decide if he really didn't want to work with her, of he simply didn't like being backed into a corner.

In the end, the answer was, in part, the same as it had always been. "No," he admitted. "At least not all the time, at any rate." And definitely not so long as they continued to insult her talent by dressing her up like a porn star before each session. Honestly, though he knew why she'd made the choice she'd made— and he really didn't blame her—he still didn't see how she stood it.

Then again, who was he to judge? He'd never walked in her shoes. In a similar situation, who was to say he wouldn't don a thong and let them dub him The Bare-Assed Baker?

"Then there's your answer, I'm afraid," Rupert told him. "If you don't want to work with her, then there's nothing left for you to do. Let her agent take care of it. If she's got a halfway decent one, then they'll be able to handle it."

Philip wished he could be reassured, but didn't find Rupert's advice the least bit comforting. In fact, he felt like a selfish ass, which was precisely the way Spencer had counted on him feeling. If Philip had to guess, he imagined that Spencer had caught

wind of rumors which correctly paired him up with
Carrie. It wasn't as though they'd made a big secret
about their relationship. Hell, though they hadn't
specifically said anything about it, he knew any fool
could watch their shows—particularly the last two—
and put the pieces together.

Philip swore. That bastard, he thought again. Of
all the scheming underhanded nerve.

"What happens if I bail out of my contract?"

"Aside from the fact that you'll never work in
your desired field again, nothing, I suppose," Rupert
said lightly, as though ending his career wasn't a big
deal. "What was Carrie's reaction?" his agent asked.

Philip stilled, drawing a blank. "Er…I don't
know."

"What do you mean you don't know?" Rupert
asked, almost threateningly. "She was there with
you, right? What did she say?"

Philip dialed back his memory, replayed the scene
in Spencer's office. "I, uh…"

Rupert heaved a long-suffering sigh. "Don't tell
me that you went off half-cocked and didn't even
give her a chance to speak? To defend herself. Tell
me that you care enough about her to give her the
benefit of the doubt, not just get pissed off and storm
out, leaving her alone with that controlling little asshole who is presently trying to ruin both of your ca-

reers. Tell me you didn't do that, Philip," Rupert repeated wearily, his voice depressingly resigned. "Tell me you've got sense enough to see that this girl isn't anything like Sophie."

Philip wheeled his car into his driveway, rolled to an abrupt stop, then shifted into Park. His big empty house loomed before him. The import of what he'd just done—the mistake he'd just made—settled like the weight of the world upon his shoulders. He'd done exactly what Rupert had just said.

Was guilty of all of the above.

And worse, he realized, his belly filling with a numbing sort of dread. He'd assumed that if he said no—if he refused to work with her—that she'd never forgive him and end it with him. Discard him. Stop caring. His throat tightened.

So he'd very neatly ended it with her first—in front of a smug-faced Spencer, no less—in order to beat her to the punch.

He was the bastard, Philip thought.

He massaged the bridge of his nose, felt his sinuses burn. "I've, uh… I've got to go," he said, totally distracted by the horrific mistake he'd made.

"Do you want me to come over?" Rupert offered, evidently still his friend despite his abuse and stupidity.

"No, but thanks."

"I don't have any plans," he assured him. "We'll make a night of it. Really, it's no prob—"

"I appreciate it, Rupert, but I think I'm going to have to figure out how to deal with this one on my own."

"Call me if you need me," he said. A moment later, he disconnected, leaving Philip completely on his own.

A bitter smile curled his lips. Alone again, he thought. The running theme in his life.

But this time he had no one to blame but himself.

14

"Do you want to tell me what's wrong, or am I going to have to tie you to this tree?" April hissed into Carrie's ear.

"It's not good wedding conversation," Carrie told her, hurrying around to make sure that dishes were replenished when needed. Furthermore, if she talked about it—or even thought about it, for that matter—she'd cry.

Just as she had last night.

April determinedly dogged her steps. "I don't care if it's good wedding conversation or not. The wedding is over. Technically, this is the reception."

Carrie picked a stray strawberry which had inadvertently fallen off the fruit tray from the table and popped it into her mouth. "Semantics," she said. "Seriously," she told her, pausing to look into April's worried green eyes. "I can't talk about it right now." She gestured toward Frankie, who was presently posing for pictures with her husband. "This is her day. I'm not ruining it for her."

And she meant it. As soon as this was over, she'd go home and bawl her eyes out, lick her wounds in private. But she *would not* be the cause of any unhappiness or distress on Frankie's big day.

April winced, her gaze softening with sympathy. "Later then, okay? I'm here for you." She reached out and squeezed Carrie's hand. The sweet gesture momentarily made her eyes burn.

"Thanks," Carrie told her. "I, uh... I appreciate it."

Rubbing a hand over her hugely pregnant belly, Zora carefully negotiated the terrain beneath the tree and waddled over. A fond smile curved her lips as she gestured toward Frankie. "She's beautiful, isn't she?"

Frankie, positively glowing in a beautiful white dress, and Ross, her handsome groom had officially tied the knot. Frankie hadn't wanted her abusive father at the wedding, so when it came to the point in the ceremony where the pastor asked who was giving her away, the three of them had stepped forward and in unison said, "We do."

The weather had cooperated, affording them an unseasonably cool summer day and the shade beneath the huge, towering branches proved especially nice.

April and Ben had come out early and strung hundreds of clear crystals in various shapes and sizes from the branches, and multifaceted beams of light illuminated the area with an almost fantastical fairy-tale feel. Soft jazz played from carefully hidden speakers and the occasional confused bird would swoop through, garnering a laugh from the small, intimate crowd.

Carrie's catering had been a huge hit, but the ultimate payoff had been Frankie's reaction to the hummingbird. She'd gasped, then a broken sob of happiness had erupted from her throat and she'd cried.

"It's the most beautiful, most perfect cake I have ever seen," she'd said. "I knew leaving everything up to you guys was the best way to go." Then she'd hugged each of them in turn, Zora more difficultly because her belly got in the way.

"She is gorgeous," Carrie said, gazing fondly at Frankie and Ross. Her heart ached for that sort of happiness, the kind that she'd foolishly imagined she might have had with Philip.

Clearly, that had been a pipe dream.

The first sign of trouble—the blameless sort, dammit, because she hadn't done anything wrong—and he'd cut and run without even affording her the courtesy of defending herself. She knew Philip had issues—had gleaned enough about his childhood to understand that he had justifiable abandonment concerns—but, call her crazy, she'd honestly thought that she'd gotten through to him. That she'd managed to worm her way into his affections despite his fear of potential heartache.

In short, she'd thought she was special…and she'd thought wrong.

Last night Carrie had kept expecting him to call or come by, to come to his senses and apologize for lumping her into the same opportunistic category as that witch who'd purposely stolen his last show.

She wasn't her, dammit.

As the seconds had slipped into minutes and minutes into hours, she'd realized that he wasn't going to do either.

She'd finished Frankie's spread, worked on the cake, then had quietly sobbed when she'd applied the various stems, leaves and buds Philip had made. Curiously enough she'd walked out of Spencer's office—without a job, no less, because she'd quit before she'd work for another Martin and clearly Spencer was a candidate in the making—and hadn't shed a tear. She'd calmly gathered her things in the privacy of her dressing room and hadn't so much as sniffled. Hoover's happy dance when she'd walked through the door yesterday afternoon had almost made her crumble—bless his little heart, her little dog loved her even when no one else did—but in the end she'd held it together.

But let her come across a couple of sugared cake decorations Philip had helped her with, and the damned floodgates had broken. She supposed because they'd represented so much more. The future she'd hoped they'd had, the easy companionship they'd shared while they'd worked together, and the sweet beautiful love they'd made in her kitchen after they'd finished. Though she knew it was stupid, Carrie hadn't applied all of them to Frankie's cake. She'd kept a small, delicate bud as a tortuous memento of what might have been.

"April, do you think you could work some magic with your husband to speed up the photo process?" Zora asked conversationally.

April shot her a look. "Sure. Is the heat starting to get to you?"

"No, but my water just broke, I should probably get to the hospital and I'm not having this baby without Frankie."

It took a second for Zora's matter-of-fact statement to penetrate, but when it did both Carrie and April squealed and sprang into action. "You're in labor?" April gasped. "Now?"

Tate was at Zora's side in less than three seconds.

"What's going on?" he asked, carefully reading his wife's face.

"Her water broke," Carrie told him.

Tate's eyes widened and slow smile moved across his lips. Zora confirmed Carrie's pronouncement with a soft nod and the two of them shared an excitedly tender look.

Frankie hiked up her dress and, veil bobbing, husband hot on her heels, ran to Zora's side. "What? Did I just hear someone say that your water broke?"

Zora nodded. "Yes."

Tate started herding his wife toward the car and the rest of guests followed them, trying to keep up with what was going on.

Frankie squealed delightedly, then her face blanked and she glared at Zora. "Have you been having contractions?" she asked accusingly.

"Since five o'clock this morning," Zora confirmed.

Huffing it along right beside her, Frankie yelped in frustration. "Five o'clock! *And you came here? Have you lost your mind?*"

"I couldn't miss your wedding. We had to give you away. Besides, first time labor takes a notoriously long time."

"Be that as it may, that's completely reckless! I've read the books."

Hurrying along as well, April jumped into the fray. "She's right. We're almost an hour from town. How far apart are your contractions? Have you been timing them?"

Tate opened Zora's car door, reached across and quickly buckled her in. "Six minutes," she said, slightly out of breath. "We've got plenty of time."

Carrie thought she heard Tate say something which sounded suspiciously like "stubborn know-it-all."

"I heard that," Zora admonished, shooting her husband a glare as he slid behind the wheel of the car. She glanced nervously at her friends and an uncharacteristic flash of something akin to fear momentarily shadowed her ordinarily unflappable gaze. "Y'all are coming right?"

"Of course," Frankie said briskly, and Carrie and April echoed the sentiment.

Tate quickly maneuvered the car from the side of the road and took off. Frankie glanced at Ross. "Do you mind if we're a little late leaving for our honeymoon?" she asked anxiously, clearly torn between her new husband and her old friend.

"Not at all, babe. Whatever makes you happy."

Frankie beamed at him and kissed his cheek. "That's why I love you."

"What about all this stuff?" April asked, gesturing toward the tables, chairs, food and decorations. "We can't just all take off."

"We'll take care of it," her father said, immediately stepping forward to volunteer himself and Davy, Ben's father, as clean-up crew.

"Are you sure, Dad?" she asked.

"Certainly, honey. Go be with your friend."

"The coolers and things are all in my SUV," Carrie said, pointing out another problem.

"Leave it," Davy said. "We'll get it back into town."

"You can ride with us," April told her. "We'll drop you off at home when we leave the hospital."

Satisfied that all was in order, Carrie, April and Frankie gathered their purses and the hems of their gowns and took off across the field.

"Slow down," Ross admonished his wife, ambling along behind her. "You're carrying my unborn child."

Frankie beamed at the two of them. "Can you believe it? We're having a baby!"

"I KNOW YOU'RE THERE," Rupert said. "You're like a pack animal. When you're wounded you burrow. Pick up the phone." Rupert paused. "Dammit, Philip. I need to talk to you. I got a call from Joyce last night and there's something you should know."

Philip was tempted to pick up the phone at this news, but ultimately resisted. He wasn't in the mood to talk to anyone, not even Rupert, though he knew his friend had his best interests at heart.

He'd been unforgivably stupid, then had compounded matters by being a coward to boot.

He should have called her, gone to her—done something—but after the mess he'd made of everything, facing her had simply been too hard. He felt like a royal class fool and knew he'd need to do something extraordinary to fix it and get back into her good graces.

Provided he even could.

Rupert's exasperated sigh hissed into his answering machine. "Fine," he said. "We'll do it your way. Yesterday after you left, Carrie quit. Completely. She—" A long annoying beep sounded as Philip snatched the phone from the receiver.

"She did *what?*" he exploded.

"Ah," Rupert said knowingly. "So you are there. Excellent."

"She quit?" he asked, his heart racing into an irregular rhythm. His mouth went dry. Sweet Jesus... She couldn't have. What on earth would possess her to— Philip raked a hand over his face. "Tell me everything," he demanded. "Everything that you know."

"I would have told you a lot sooner if you'd answered the damned phone. I take it you haven't talked her, then?"

"No," Philip admitted, ashamed.

"You beautiful fool!" Rupert snapped. "Why the hell not?"

"Just tell me why she quit," Philip demanded. "Please."

"She quit because she said she didn't appreciate Spencer's tactics, said it reminded her of her former boss. Her agent has already issued a check for the buyout on the remaining time on her contract." He paused. "She's finished with them."

And out of a job, because he'd refused to work with her. Guilt settled over him like a heavy blanket and his stomach rolled.

"It never occurred to me that you wouldn't call her," Rupert said. "I thought you knew she was no Sophie."

He had. He'd merely forgotten it at a crucial moment.

Philip swore. "I can't believe she did that," he said, still flabbergasted. Admittedly, he'd thought Spencer was a high-handed bastard, but he'd never entertained quitting or buying out his contract.

Philip harrumphed with disgust. And he'd once thought *she'd* sold out.

"I realize that I may not be the best agent, Philip, and I'm certain there have been times when I've given you faulty advice. But I know this—Carrie Robbins is the girl for you, and you're the biggest nitwit in the northern hemisphere if you don't go fix this."

He was right, Philip thought, every cell in his body belatedly infusing with determination.

It was time to be a man—the man for her, if she'd still have him.

15

"Oh, my gosh," Frankie whispered reverently. "Look at her," she said. Her eyes misted with tears. "Oh, Zora, she's beautiful."

The tired but still gorgeous new mother slid a finger over her newborn daughter's downy red head. "We think so," she said softly.

Tate's eyes were slightly red-rimmed, but if you asked him he'd deny that seeing his wife bring their baby into the world had brought him to tears. Allergies, no doubt would get the blame. He presently lay curled up on the bed next to his wife, already on guard in his role as the protector of their family.

The sight of them made Carrie's eyes mist with tears. Gad, she felt like all she'd done today was cry. She'd cried over Philip, cried for Frankie, and was now crying for Zora and their new baby.

Predictably, within five minutes of being in the car on the way to the hospital, April had started grilling her about Philip. Or more specifically, what had happened with Philip. Carrie had related the whole sordid tale and by the end of her spiel, she'd been sobbing. Why couldn't anything ever go right for her? she'd wondered. Why did everything have to be so damned hard?

While April had thought Philip had made a stupid mistake, she didn't think it was time to write him off completely. Men didn't think like women, she'd said, and sometimes it took them a little longer to come to the same conclusion a woman would reach in less than a quarter of the time. According to her, they were linear thinkers when it came to almost every matter, except those of an emotional nature.

Since she'd imparted all of this with an air of firsthand experience, Carrie was almost inclined to believe her, but at this point, she was honestly too mentally and emotionally exhausted to think about it anymore.

As for Spencer and his threat, April had wholeheartedly agreed that Carrie should have quit. Having another boss like Martin was on her life's-too-short list. She didn't have any idea what she'd do now, but she knew that whatever it was would be better than being beholden to another asshole. Something would come along. It always did. In the meantime she'd rat-holed enough money to see her through for a little while.

"Well," Frankie said, still clad in her wedding dress. "What are we naming our new CHiC?"

Zora smiled and looked up at her husband. "You can do the honors," she said.

Tate cleared his throat. "Ladies, meet Caroline Francesca Dawn."

April cocked her head, Frankie's brow puckered in slight confusion and a bubble of joy burst in Carrie's chest.

"For her honorary aunts," Zora explained. "She's named for all of you."

Frankie gasped and April's hand darted to her throat. "Thank you," April breathed. "I—I'm honored. I didn't know you even remembered my middle name."

"I didn't," Zora confessed. She grinned. "Your husband told me."

Frankie darted a curious look at Carrie. "You're a Caroline?" she asked.

"I am."

"You don't look like a Caroline."

"I know," Carrie told her. "That's why I shortened it."

Ben moved in behind April and wrapped his arms around her waist. She leaned instinctively against him, her face wreathed in a contented smile. "That's an awfully big name for such a tiny little girl," he remarked.

Zora gazed lovingly at her new baby. "I'm not worried. She's gonna have the personality to pull it off."

Carrie grinned. She didn't doubt that for a moment. "We should go," she finally said. "It's late and new parents need their rest."

Frankie let go a sigh. "She's right." She glanced at her watch, then darted a look at her new husband over her shoulder. "If we hurry we can still make our flight."

"Go, go," Zora shooed. "Don't miss your plane."

After much hugging and more tears and promises to visit the next day, the five of them finally wandered out into the hall. Carrie, April and Ben were in the middle of wishing Frankie and Ross a happy honeymoon when the back of Carrie's neck prickled with awareness.

Frankie's shrewd gaze darted over Carrie's shoulder. "Were you expecting your Brit?" she asked.

Her belly did a backflip and her pulse began to pound so hard she felt slightly faint. "No."

"Well, he's here."

Evidently feeling protective, April scooted in closer to her and darted a mutinous haughty glare at Philip. "Do you want me to run him off?" she asked.

Ben and Ross shared a look. "Do we need to kick someone's ass?" Ben wanted to know.

"Ha. CHiCs do their own ass-kickin'," Frankie told them. "I don't know what he did, babe, but go yank a knot in it for him," she said in threatening carrying tones. "You'll feel better."

"Carrie?" Philip finally asked. "C-could I have a word please?" he asked tentatively.

Bracing herself with a shuddering breath, Carrie finally turned around. Looking more mussed and frazzled than she'd ever seen him, Philip stood a few feet from her, an agonizingly anxious expression on his face, which unfortunately made her aching heart squeeze. Even completely in the wrong, he still managed to affect her.

He pushed a hand through his hair, looked away, then found her gaze once more. "If you'll just give me a moment of your time, I promise I—"

"It'll have to be a moment," Carrie told him, walking toward him. "My friends are waiting to take me home."

His eyes widened, then, "Er…I could give you a lift," he offered hopefully.

Absolutely not. "I don't think—"

"Please," he interrupted and there was something so humble and heart-wrenching about the sincerity in his voice that Carrie finally nodded and told them not to wait for her.

"You're sure?" April asked. "We can go to the car and—"

Carrie shook her head. "I'll be fine."

Frankie gave her a squeeze. "Call me if you need to."

"You're going on your honeymoon," Carrie reminded her, touched by her friend's unfailing support.

"Ah, hell. We've been on a honeymoon since we met," Frankie told her, her dark brown eyes drifting over to her husband. "This is more like a vacation…with extra sex."

Carrie chuckled despite herself. "Have a good time."

Finally the hall cleared and only she and Philip were left standing there. Philip shoved his hands into his pockets and his silvery gaze moved over her face, lingered around her eyes, which were no doubt puffy and swollen. "I've been looking for you today," he finally managed.

Carrie didn't speak. She wasn't going to make this easy on him. He'd been wrong. She didn't owe him the courtesy of a single word.

When it was obvious that she didn't intend to respond, Philip let go a small breath. "I went by your house, then remembered the wedding when you weren't there. It took me a little over an hour to find the tree, but by the time I'd arrived, there were only a couple of guys left loading things into your car. They directed me here, said that Zora had gone into labor. Has she delivered?" Philip asked.

"A couple of hours ago. A little girl."

That faintly crooked smile appeared. "Oh, good. Both are well?"

Carrie nodded. Then waited.

Philip hesitated worriedly. "Carrie, I…" He let go a heavy breath, shook his head. "I, uh— I don't even know where to begin."

She started to suggest with an apology, but held her tongue. He'd put her through total hell. He'd underestimated her, embarrassed her, hurt her feelings and ultimately broken her heart yesterday. He'd lifted her up this week, then dropped her without the least amount of provocation on her part.

If this was hard for him, then it should be, dammit. Though a part of her ached for him—knew that he was trying to fix things—the wounded part of her knew that Philip needed to do this on his own, without any prodding or help on her part. Forgiveness wasn't cheap and if asking for it was too high a price for him, then, much as it would hurt her, she didn't want him.

His gaze tangled with hers. "I'm sorry," he said, his voice a mix sincerity and despair.

Her silly heart grew cautiously hopeful, but she managed to restrain herself from jumping into his arms.

"This would be easier if you'd done something wrong, if you could take even a small part of the blame," he said. He shook his head, offered a helpless smile and shrugged. "But you can't because you didn't do anything wrong. You didn't leap to inaccurate conclusions or cut me to the quick as a result of that stupidity. And you did what I didn't have the guts to do—you quit."

Bad news for the ice cream companies, Carrie thought, because it didn't look as if they'd be getting her brokenhearted business. She saw something in Philip's gaze that she'd been waiting for her entire adult life. Something as precious as love, but which didn't often get the attention it deserved because, in her opinion, you couldn't have one without the other.

Respect.

"I can't believe you did that," Philip told her, seemingly awed. "You have more character and strength, more intelligence and integrity than any woman I have ever met."

Damn it all to hell, she was going to cry again.

Nervous energy made her want to bounce on the balls of her feet.

"And I'm in love with you," he said, delivering the coup de grâce. His woefully familiar silvery eyes searched hers. "Say something," he implored. "Anything. *Thanks, but no, thanks. Keep your heart, Philip. Go to hell, Philip. Sod off, Philip.*" He grimaced, inclined his head. "Or, *I accept your apology and I love you, too, Philip.*" He pretended to consider it. "Actually, if I'm to get a say, the last option works best for me."

It did for her, too, Carrie thought. She felt a smile slide around her lips and her heart warmed with equal parts of hope and happiness. She moved forward, slid her arms around his waist and placed a reverent kiss against his heart. She heard Philip's breath catch and a relieved sigh leak out.

"I accept your apology and I love you, too, Philip."

Smiling, he drew back and looked down at her upturned face. "See, now. That was quite efficient, wasn't it?"

Then he lowered his head and efficiently kissed the hell out of her.

Epilogue

Eight and a half months later...

CARRIE SIPPED HER CLUB SODA and fondly watched her husband of six months play a game of pool with Ben, Ross and Tate across the room. From the looks of things, Tate and Ross were sharing pregnant-wife-and-new-mother tips, and thankfully, Ben and Philip were clinging to the advice.

As well they should, since both she and April were pregnant and Frankie was due practically any day now.

Occasionally passersby would pause outside the windows of the Blue Monkey Pub and stare at the festivities inside. No doubt trying to figure out why anyone would host a baby shower at a bar, Carrie thought. Oh, well. It wasn't anyone else's business. This little pub had played an unwittingly significant role in their lives and somehow it only seemed fitting that they celebrate impending births here.

Frankie held up the little pink dress that Carrie had picked up in a specialty shop on the Isle of Wight—Philip's home away from home, which Carrie had fallen instantly in love with—and smiled delightedly. "This is beautiful, Carrie. Thanks!"

Caroline Francesca Dawn—better known as Frannie—gurgled contentedly in her mother's lap. "Could we move along to the big announcement, please?" Zora asked. "I want to know what you're naming my future godchild."

Frankie grinned. "What makes you think my big announcement has anything to do with what we're naming this baby?"

"Intuition," Zora replied archly.

"Well, for once you're wrong." She put a hand on the side of her big belly. "If I told you what I planned on naming this baby, then I'd be telling you the sex of the child, and like you," she needled significantly, "I'm not giving that up."

"But you know?" Carrie asked.

Frankie merely smiled. "Of course."

April goggled at her. "Then why on earth didn't you tell us so that we'd know whether to buy for a boy or a girl?" She glanced at the huge pile forming on the table next to Frankie. "Who's going to haul back the stuff you won't be able to use?"

Practical as always, Carrie thought, smiling at her

friend. But she was right. Zora purposely avoided finding out the sex of her baby because she'd wanted to be surprised at the birth. But if Frankie already knew…

Intrigued, Carrie paused and considered her friend. What on earth was up with her?

April leaned over. "Have you thought about what you're naming your little bambino?" she asked. "Firmed up any first choices?"

Since she and Philip had married beneath the tree as well—then had later gone back and honeymooned there, which was when she'd conceived—Carrie and Philip were considering a couple of names significant to the occasion. "Actually, yes. Rowan, if it's a girl. Ash, if it's a boy."

April eyes sparkled and she chewed the inside of her cheek. "Tree names, eh?"

Carrie shared the *significant* part. "What about you and Ben? What have y'all come up with?"

"Willow for a girl, and we were also considering Ash for a boy," she added with a slight wince. "It'll be a race to the delivery room to claim that one, won't it?" April teased. She and April were due mere days apart.

Carrie felt a grin tug at her lips. "That tree's seen a lot of action, hasn't it?"

April chuckled. "It would seem so." She paused. "How are things at the restaurant?"

"Couldn't be better," Carrie told her. Philip had bought out his contract with the network as well and, since both of them had been out of work and wondering what to do next, Frankie had glibly suggested that a restaurant would be the perfect way to capitalize on both their talents and their notoriety.

She'd been right.

Penny's, so named in honor of the little sister Philip had lost, had been booked solid for the first six months before the doors had even opened. It was the best of both worlds, Carrie thought. She and Philip been able to combine the art of cooking with the drama of their personalities and the result had been a successful restaurant which was garnering worldwide attention. Her gaze slid to her husband once more and a bolt of pure joy landed squarely in her chest. She couldn't be happier.

Frankie tapped her spoon against her glass, garnering everyone's attention. Ross looked up, took that as his cue and moved in behind his wife and placed his hands on her shoulders.

Carrie smiled as she felt Philip do the same. She bent her head back and offered her mouth for a kiss, then watched as the other two roosters quickly ambled over and found their CHiCs.

"I promised you all a big announcement," Frankie said, her sly gaze sweeping the room. "And I don't think that it's going to disappoint. Some of you thought we planned to reveal a name tonight," she said, looking pointedly at Zora. Her gaze then darted to April and Carrie. "And some of you Type-A anal-retentive wonder girls have been puzzled over the fact that, even though Ross and I know the sex of this baby—" again she placed her hand over the left side of her belly "—we didn't disclose that information and made you all buy gifts for both a girl and a boy."

Carrie's eyes widened, she gasped and covered her hand with her mouth.

Frankie grinned at her. "That's because we're not having one baby—we're having two! A boy *and* a girl, Quenton Ross, Jr., and Liliana Grace, respectively." She nodded primly as the room erupted with squeals and shouts of joy.

"You sneak!" Zora told her. "How long have you known this?"

"Since my fourth month."

"And you didn't tell?" she asked incredulously. "How could you not tell?" she demanded, flabbergasted.

Frankie and Ross shared a tender look. "It was our little secret," she said. Her eyes twinkled. "Besides, this was a lot more fun."

Carrie shook her head and chuckled, her gaze drifting from happy couple to happy couple. Philip's warm breath suddenly breezed against her ear, causing a shiver of heat to pulse through her. "That was certainly interesting," he said. "Never a dull moment, eh?"

Ben heard him and simply laughed. "Not in this hen house," he said laughingly.

"Hey," April scolded. "We might be nesting now, but don't ever forget that we're CHiCs at heart."

"Hear, hear," Carrie seconded, and raised her glass. Zora's and Frankie's soon joined the fray. "To Chicks in Charge," Zora said softly, their customary toast, and they all happily echoed the sentiment.

Blaze

**It might be the wrong bed,
but he's definitely the right man!**

Catch these stories of the wrong circumstances bringing
together the right couple:

Rock My World
by Cindi Myers,
November 2005

All I Want…
by Isabel Sharpe,
December 2005

Anticipation
by Jennifer LaBrecque,
January 2006

Available wherever books are sold.

HARLEQUIN *Blaze*

Three of Harlequin Blaze's hottest authors brought you
the **RED LETTER NIGHTS** anthology this November.

Now get ready for more as each of these authors
writes her own steamy tale....

GIVE ME FEVER
by **Karen Anders**

On sale December 2005

When Tally Addison's brother goes missing,
she knows who to turn to—gorgeous cop
Christien Castille. Only, when she and Christien
stumble into a search for hidden treasure,
she discovers she's already found hers...in him.

Coming in 2006...
GOES DOWN EASY by Alison Kent;
Book #225, January 2006

GOING, GOING, GONE by Jeanie London;
Book #231, February 2006